BLACKDAW COTTAGE

PHILIP DENT

Matador
5 Weir Road
Kibworth Beauchamp
Leicester LE8 0LQ, UK
Tel: (+44) 116 279 2299
Fax: (+44) 116 279 2277
Email: books@troubador.co.uk
Web: www.troubador.co.uk/matador

ISBN 978 1848766 556

British Library Cataloguing in Publication Data.
A catalogue record for this book is available from the British Library.

Printed and bound in the UK by TJ International, Padstow, Cornwall

Typeset in 10.5pt Palatino by Troubador Publishing Ltd, Leicester, UK

Matador is an imprint of Troubador Publishing Ltd

BLACKDAW COTTAGE

For the blossoming generation:
Lauren, Anna, Lucy, Holly

CHAPTER 1

1960s

Children all love to play, and the heavy snowfall that had closed the village school early for Christmas provided the perfect opportunity. But snow brings with it danger, dazzling young minds and luring children into unsuspecting perils – perils that spirited children are oblivious to and unable to resist.

Piercing screams and excitable laughter echoed through the village throughout the entire morning, reminding the rural community of the impending festivities – if any reminder was indeed needed. Images of the children at play deepened the lines on the weathered faces of elderly residents, looking upon them from the comfort of cosy homes.

Snowmen had sprung up overnight as eagerly as mushrooms in the damp grass of balmy autumnal months. Children moulded snowballs and snow-fight play ensued; but when fingers numbed from the cold recoiled at again being plunged into the white crystals, one activity was abandoned in favour of another, and the children towed each other about the village green on makeshift sledges. The enchanting scene was prevalent in the villages and towns throughout the country on that cold December day.

The hessian curtain draped over the window of the cottage in the forest was drawn aside, and the white-bearded face of an elderly gentleman looked out through the tangle of cobwebs. He frowned, uttering a grunt of displeasure. The toll of advancing years and the hardships he had endured

– willingly, it has to be said – had set the corners of his mouth in a downward droop, like the sad face of a sad clown. But Bentley was not sad; the solitary old man was happy living in his quaint cottage in the depths of the forest.

He was dressing for a journey. Already wearing a ragged heavy overcoat, he pulled the balaclava he played with in his hands over his head, leaving only his eyes and weather-reddened nose visible – and drifts of white whiskers. He again glanced out into the cold forest, but turned swiftly from it, nipping his eyelids tight. The glare from the low-lying winter sun stung his eyes.

The cat, meowing repeatedly at his feet, rubbed the length of her body along his legs, before turning and repeating the procedure from the opposite direction. Bentley smiled and reopened his eyes.

'No point you fussing, soft thing,' he said in a voice that squeaked when his smile mutated into laughter. 'Got to go to the village, Elsa. Need more provisions before more snow comes. The sky lies. I feel it in my aching old bones.' He let go of the curtain and limped from the window as if to prove a point. But what did a cat know or care about his rheumatic bones, or about the snow for that matter? All Elsa cared for was that she was warm and well fed and had a friendly knee on which to lay her head.

Bentley lifted the knapsack up from the floor and slung it on his back; he turned and glanced to the fire, having banked it up earlier – smothered the flames with ash – in the hope that the fire would remain alive and keep his home warm until he returned. Thick white smoke wormed a tortured path up the chimney breast, fighting against a persistent down-draft. Satisfied, Bentley turned and shuffled towards the door under the cat's inquisitive eyes. The cat turned also and trod softly to the fireside where she sat licking her forepaws, glancing occasionally to him. The old man watched his loyal feline companion lay down and stretch out on the warm hearth.

'Aye, you know best, Elsa. You know where it's warm. Too cold out today. Too darn cold for cats. Too darn cold by far.' He chuckled. The contented feline cast her waning gaze in his direction once more and then closed her eyes.

A bitter wind greeted the old man as he opened the door. After hesitating, he took a deep breath and then stepped out into the cold morning air, closing the door quickly behind him. He adjusted his clothing, glanced briefly to the smoke rising from the crooked metal chimney that protruded through the roof of his cottage, and then set out in the direction of the village, striding with unexpected vigour across the crisp ankle-deep snow.

Dinnertime approached and the children, wet and cold from playing in the snow, made off at intervals for their homes. The prospect of a hot meal and the chance to restore feeling to fingers and toes, chilled beyond numbness and turning painful, had lessened the attraction of the snow.

Once the euphoria had faded and animated chatter of the morning's exploits had quietened, three children and a dog remained in a huddle on the village green. Their busy lips expelled misty breaths into the midday air. Of what did they speak?

CHAPTER 2

1690s

Grief-stricken mourners strode wearily into the cold, wet churchyard, walking without speaking until reaching the newly-dug grave. They shuffled around its four sides and stood staring into its gloomy depths, watching as the tiny wooden coffin, with its luckless occupant sealed inside, succumbed to the insatiable earth. Hands clasped tight in prayer trembled, and cold lips quivered amid much sniffing and weeping as voices, tremulous and breaking, pleaded with the Lord to take better care of the infant whose visit to earth had all too soon ended. They prayed, too, that Alice might be the last to fall victim to the plague, the cruel plague that had blighted the lives of so many. But in their hearts they knew that Alice Mayhew would not be the last.

The coffin shuddered to a stop and Alice's short journey was over. Soil, released from unwilling hands, pattered a hallowed lament upon the coffin lid. The girl's mother could withstand the torture no more; her legs buckled and she collapsed onto the earth, wailing, begging the Lord to take her too and reunite her with her poor departed children.

Teetering precariously over the edge of the grave, she appeared about to topple in when rough hands seized her ankles and drew her back. Shrieks of protest violated the silence and the men set her free. Undeterred, Joan Mayhew scurried back to the grave of her child on her hands and knees, bemoaning the injustice of her miserable existence.

The burly gravedigger, leaning his bulk on a spade,

looked scornfully upon the grieving mother – his dispassionate gait owing much to the procession of misery he had witnessed over the years – shaking his head and dislodging the rain from his brow. With disdainful eyes, he then glanced heavenwards while feet, encased in laceless boots, shifted slowly in the sticky earth. He returned his gaze earthward, yanked the spade from the earth and thrust it into the soil piled high around the grave. Stones dislodged by petulant action danced upon the coffin lid. Grimacing uneasily, the gravedigger surveyed the mourners' faces, withdrew the soil-laden implement and cast its load into the grave, before glancing again to the sobbing crowd. A grin curled the corners of his lips and, after propping the spade shaft against his thighs, he lifted both hands to his mouth and spat into each palm. Rubbing them together while eyeing the mourners, before picking up his spade, bending his back low and setting about his labour, shovelling the earth, stones and severed tree roots back into the dark hole. 'Speak now or be forever quieted,' the clangour seemed to beseech.

Alice Mayhew was no more. Prayers uttered amid sobbing pitched higher and louder, drowning the sound of the gravedigger's spade repeatedly violating the earth.

Gabriel Mayhew seized his opportunity; he clambered upon a makeshift platform, anxiously seeking his wife. He found her lying on her stomach upon the muddied earth, overcome by grief, her body convulsing and her fingers curling and unfurling. Gabriel inhaled deeply, he drew the back of a clenched fist across his mouth and turned to the stooped figures shuffling away.

'Halt, people, I beseech you, wait!' He called out through tremulous lips. The departing mourners halted and turned. 'Are we to do nothing?' He continued. His eyes were wide and wild, his breathing heavy. The mourners listened in silence, focusing upon him. 'Be not afraid, you people. Be brave. Protect your children while they yet live. Do not do as I and wait not for the curse of Murdac to strike. For then it is too late.'

The reviled name spoken out loud drew gasps from the crowd, heightening their fears, giving rise to questioning exchanges. But what could be done against the will of the Lord?

CHAPTER 3

The cloudless sky stretched as far as the eye could see in every direction, but the bright winter sun provided little warmth. Excitable children, though, are immune from the cold, and to the three friends the sub-zero temperature was barely noticeable. For the umpteenth time, Ruth, Abigail and Morton set off down the steep slope on their flimsy wooden sledge, fast and precarious over the snow. It lay at an ideal depth for sledging; deep enough to allow the conveyance to glide easily over it, but not too deep to ensnare the runners and slow it down.

The thrill, intermingled with fear, bestowing a delicious sensation that animated the three friends as the sledge sped faster and faster down the hill, bouncing over ridges and leaping into the air, skewing this way and that. After veering suddenly left, Ruth and Morton were catapulted from it; over and over they rolled in the powdery, cold snow. Sputnik, Ruth's Jack Russell terrier, was eager to join in the fun and scurried after them on its short, strong legs, barking furiously. Abigail, the least experienced in the art of sledging, had somehow managed to cling on; and with the load lightened, the sledge sped faster than ever down the steep incline. Ruth and Morton, rendered insensible from giggling, rose from the snow together and watched their friend.

'I'll race you,' Ruth said suddenly, setting off after the runaway sledge. 'Hold on tight, Abigail!'

Morton looked on with envy, hoping that Abigail would fall from it too. But she did not fall off, and the sledge came to a halt at the foot of the hill. Abigail, relieved that her moment of terror was over, but reluctant to show it, dismounted and turned to her approaching friends.

'Did you see? I was going really fast, wasn't I?'

'Fast!' Mocked Morton. 'That was nothing. I can go faster than any girl can, much faster.'

'Oh, sure,' responded Ruth, sardonically.

'Bet you can't,' cut in Abigail.

'Can.'

'Right then, Morton Rymer, we'll see how clever you are,' said Ruth, striding towards the sledge, picking the towrope up from the snow and dragging the sledge back up the steep hill. Abigail, eager to assist, hurried to her side.

The three children were suitably dressed to combat the cold on that bitter December day. They wore extra layers of woollens beneath heavy overcoats, wellington boots to keep their feet dry, thick woollen gloves on their hands and scarves that were wrapped several times around slender necks. Mrs Markson, Abigail's mother, normally forbade her daughter from playing out in her red duffel coat, but since it was the warmest she possessed, today she had insisted on her wearing it. Ruth's dark woollen overcoat looked as though full value had been already obtained from it, bearing patches of different shades of brown where her mother had mended it. The hoods of the girls' coats were pulled over knitted woollen hats, leaving little bare flesh for the frost to torment. Morton appeared burdened within the long black overcoat that he wore, being several sizes too large for his small frame – he was shorter than both girls – the ragged hem flapped only inches above his ankles. A dark blue balaclava, knitted some time ago by his mother, kept his head and neck warm.

After reaching the summit of the hill, Morton scrambled eagerly onto the sledge:

'Watch me,' he said, shuffling into position on it. 'You'll

see if I can't go faster than you, Abigail Markson.'

Abigail remained tight-lipped, smiling wryly and watching.

'Ready?' Asked Ruth, bending and pushing the sledge before Morton had the opportunity to reply.

'Wait!' He yelled, grabbing hold of the wet cord. Ruth ignored him and kicked harder. The sledge gathered speed quickly, almost unbalancing her as raced from her reach.

'Look at me!' Shouted Morton, turning round, turning swiftly back. 'I'm going faster already,' he boasted. 'Said I would, didn't I?'

The sledge sped away down the ridged hill, skewing one way and then the other, bouncing off a furrow and leaping high into the air. It landed on one runner and flipped over, throwing Morton from it. He rose quickly spitting out snow, but giddy with laughter. Ruth and Abigail, laughing hysterically, joined him.

'Very clever,' began Ruth sardonically. 'But weren't you were supposed to stay on the sledge?'

'Very funny,' responded Morton, turning animated in his next breath. 'But, but did you see me, I –?'

'See you? We…' Laughter only prevented Ruth from heaping further ridicule upon him.

Morton removed a wellington boot and rested his stockinged foot upon the upturned sledge, he upturned the boot and slapped the floppy rubber sides to clear out the snow that had worked its way inside.

'Told you I could go faster… And I did,' boasted Morton, squeezing his foot back inside the boot, stamping in order to firm it.

'Well, at least I didn't fall off,' Abigail reminded him.

'You would have done if you'd been going as fast as me.'

'Sputnik!' Ruth called out. When her dog reached her

side, she bent and lifted the animal from the snow, setting him down on the sledge. 'Sit! Stay!' She bid him, as she gathered up the rope.

Sputnik had other ideas and jumped from the sledge the instant that it moved. Barking maniacally, he began circling the children again and again until he must have been dizzy.

'Stop it, Sputnik!' Ruth yelled repeatedly, until he obeyed.

Sputnik continued to bark. He rolled in the snow and wriggled around on his back, kicking his legs in the air, before scrambling to his feet, barking and growling. He lowered himself onto his forepaws, burrowed under the snow with his nose, like a pig might in mud.

Madness in animals is sometimes interpreted as a warning of impending stormy weather, but excitable children could not be expected to be aware of any such signs.

CHAPTER 4

The mourners shuffled uneasily about, whispering cautiously to each other; reckless talk they feared might provoke evil consequences. But Gabriel Mayhew seemed not to care; he watched as two men lifted his wife up from the ground. Enfeebled with grief, she flopped in their arms like a drunk, looking forlornly to her husband, as though questioning the point of living in such an unforgiving world. Gabriel turned to the mourners.

'Friends. We have suffered enough. Now is the time for action.' He paused. 'Or will you do as I, watch and hope for a miracle as your children are taken from you before your eyes? Whose child might next fall victim to the curse of Murdac?' He pointed. 'Your daughters, Rachel, Esther or Ethel?' The girls' parents stood tight-lipped, shaking their heads, but they could not hide the fear in their eyes. 'We can no longer disregard the threat to our children and look on while they perish. We must act. We must act now, today!' He shifted his vision and pointed in a different direction. 'What of your two hard-working boys, Dominic and Abraham, should they succumb to the plague? Who will plant the corn when you are old and weak?' Again he was met with silence, and Gabriel surveyed the crowd with growing animation. 'Who can I count on to join me?'

The crowd remained silent, shuffling their feet, staring with unease at the agitated speaker. Gabriel lips tightened, and then burst apart.

'Speak up, whom! Who will join me?' He paused and looked over them with growing impatience, but all remained silent. 'Damn you, cowardly fools.' He retorted spitefully. 'Go, all of you, take your children and ride to hell on the devil's back.' He turned and was about to walk away when a frail, elderly lady raised a hand and stepped forward from the crowd.

'But what can we do? Tell us, Gabriel, what?' She stood firm, staring up at him. Dressed in a ragged gown, a scarf was wrapped carelessly about her head and fell with equal disorder over her bony shoulders. She stood awaiting an answer, blinking the rain from her eyes.

'Lady,' began Gabriel, 'we must first be strong to ourselves, and we must be strong for our children. We must stand together, seek out and destroy the evil that afflicts our children.' As he returned his gaze to the crowd, his tone hardened. 'We must act now, before it's too late. Take up arms and march to Blackdaw Cottage, purge the evil that lurks among us. We must drive away, destroy the evil pair that steals the lives of our children. We must –'

'God will decide their fate.' A vociferous voice interrupted. The crowd turned to a bald-headed man forcing his way forward, waving a Bible above his head. 'God will decide our fate and our children's fate. Not you or I.'

'God!' Retorted Gabriel, shaking with rage.

'God has put the devil among us to chastise you sinners.' The pious man shouted. 'And we must pray for forgiveness, pray and the evil that blights the lives of our children will disappear like magic. And make no mistake, there *are* sinners who must be purged of their evil ways.' He pointed to Gabriel, as though accusing him of sinfulness, and then the man fell to his knees and began to pray.

'Hallelujah!' Another man shouted, falling to his knees also.

Gabriel watched with dismay as others followed, clasping their hands together and praying. Rage contorted Gabriel's face.

'Get up off your knees, fools. What use are your prayers? I prayed night and day that my children might live. God did not answer my prayers and he will not answer yours. God did not spare my children; he will not spare yours. God is impotent, a fraud. God is an image that stalks the minds of the deluded. And a prayer! False words giving rise to false hope.'

The crowd, having never before witnessed such blaspheming, gasped together. Fear and outrage maddened their eyes, but no one spoke.

'Who among you has courage?' Asked Gabriel. 'Who among you has the courage to walk with me tonight to Blackdaw Cottage?'

As he awaited an answer, the crowd glanced fitfully to each other; they eyed Gabriel, but their lips remained sealed. Then a tall gaunt man made his way forwards.

'I, Gabriel. I will join you – walk with you to Blackdaw Cottage. I'll do anything if my last surviving son might live. Isaac is all my wife and I have left of six sons and a daughter.'

The crowd gasped and prayers were hurriedly whispered. When their praying was over, they began conversing with each other, calmly at first, and then their tone hardened. Anger long repressed, born from the injustice of their suffering, surfaced. Men and women, brothers and sisters, all who had suffered, raised their hands and yelled. Within minutes every able-bodied man, woman and child voiced their desire to follow Gabriel to Blackdaw Cottage. The crowd yelled and cheered, they jeered and jumped up and down.

'God has put the devil among us to test us,' Gabriel said. 'We must show him that we are strong, that we will not be intimidated, that we are equal to his challenge. The devil and his witch must be destroyed.'

The gaunt man thrust a clenched fist in the air. 'To Blackdaw Cottage!'

'To Blackdaw Cottage!' The crowd repeated, chanting the name again and again.

'Comrades, darkness will soon be upon us,' began Gabriel. 'In one hour we must be ready –'

'To Blackdaw Cottage,' interrupted the chanting crowd.

'We must march to Blackdaw Cottage; and we must not return until the devil's lair is reduced to ashes, and the devil and his witch are writhing in the fires of hell.'

A roar from the crowd erupted; it grew louder and became increasingly frenzied. The transformation was complete: responsible men, gentle womenfolk and innocent children had turned into an angry mob, baying for the blood of fellow humans of whom they knew nothing at all.

It was as black as midnight at four o'clock on that dismal afternoon. Rain teemed relentlessly from the sky, but Gabriel and his followers did not care. Men carrying flaming lanterns led the way through the dark forest. Lightning flashed across the sky; it echoed through the forest like the cackling of demented witches. Thunder followed the like of which none had before witnessed, grumbling all about them like the hooves of stampeding buffalo. The earth trembled, but Gabriel and his followers marched fearlessly on. They drew strength from the tempest, certain that the storm was on the side of good, Heaven-sent to assist them in their duty. Evil, they sensed, would be defeated.

'Death to the devil and his witch,' the marchers chanted, again and again. Their fury seeming to rouse the storm to greater heights, driving them on through the hostile night. None would return to their homes that night until their task had been accomplished, and the Murdacs were no more.

CHAPTER 5

'Death to the devil!' Shouted Morton, racing ahead of the two girls and urging them to speed up. Only Sputnik shared his sense of urgency, bounding after him, barking excitedly. 'Death to the devil at Blackdaw Cottage.'

Running through the snow though was hard work and Morton, breathless but animated halted. Seldom was he as happy as at that moment. Living in the cramped cottage in the village with his father (his mother having walked out some years earlier) was not much fun. His dad was sometimes abusive of an evening after consuming too much alcohol in the local pub. Additionally, Mr Rymer made unreasonable demands upon his son, insisting that the chores *he* should responsible for were discharged by Morton before he was allowed out to play. Today, the opportunity to go sledging with Ruth and Abigail proved irresistible, and much of the housework remained to be done. While distracted by domestic thought, Ruth and Abigail sneaked up behind him, clutching snowballs in hands hidden behind their backs. Their giggling caused Morton to turn round, but it was too late. The girls released their snowballs, both hitting their target.

'Rotten swines,' complained Morton, brushing snow from his coat, but laughing. Ruth formed another snowball and threw it hurriedly, but Morton ducked in time and it passed over his head. Sputnik, assuming that the snowball was intended for his amusement, raced to where it fell and barked.

'Quiet, Sputnik!' Ruth bid her dog, kicking snow over him. 'Else the gamekeeper will be onto us.'

It had been Ruth's idea into walk into the forest on that

cold December afternoon, but it was Morton who had persuaded her they should walk to Blackdaw Cottage. The fact that it was another bitterly cold day did not matter to Ruth or to Morton. Only Abigail questioned their motives for straying so far from home when further blizzards had been forecast. Exercise in the countryside and surrounding woodlands was alien to the life that Abigail had so far been accustomed. Mrs Markson forbid her daughter from venturing anywhere near the forest, fearing that the 'scruffy old tramp' that she had seen in the village, and of whom she heard lived in a cottage in the forest, might do her daughter harm. Had Abigail's father not intervened, it was unlikely that she would have been granted permission that day to 'run wild with those two ragamuffins', as Mrs Markson sometimes disparagingly referred to Ruth and Morton.

The deeper into the forest the three children ventured, the more Abigail felt the cold, and the deeper she felt the cold bite into her fingers and toes, the guiltier she felt at defying her mother's wishes. Blackdaw Cottage seemed such a long way when the daylight hours were short. Ruth and Morton, though, were determined; they would walk to Blackdaw Cottage come what may, and Abigail was eventually persuaded. Even though intermittent thoughts of home, a blazing fire and her mother's cooking, caused her to dawdle and fall behind.

'Wait for me!' She called out, as she struggled to catch up. It was not easy keeping to the brisk pace of her country-bred friends, wading through ankle-deep snow in footwear she was unused to.

'Hurry then,' urged Ruth.

Hearing his mistress's voice caused Sputnik gallop to her side, wagging his tail and barking enthusiastically. 'Quiet, Sputnik!' She bid him, bending and patting her dog. 'We don't want old Vargis, the gamekeeper, chasing after us, do we?'

'Let's go home,' pleaded Abigail, after catching up. 'I'm cold and I want to go home.'

'We're not going home,' insisted Morton. 'We're going to Blackdaw Cottage, like we said. So hurry.'

'Like *you* said, you mean. And you know I can't walk fast as you in these horrid wellingtons. Why can't we go to Blackdaw Cottage another day? And I promised mum –'

'Stop moaning, will you,' Morton said. 'It'll be fun. You'll see.'

'Fun, huh! Mum said I wasn't to go near the forest where that tramp lives – and if I'm late home for tea I'll never be allowed out ever again.'

'We won't be late if you stop complaining and hurry,' said Morton.

'I told you, I can't walk as fast as you in these silly things,' she reminded him, stamping her feet petulantly.

'Oh, come on, Abigail,' pleaded Ruth, walking on. 'You'll be all right.'

'It's all right for you,' said Abigail, slipping and sliding in order to emphasise her lack of grip, her arms flailing like windmills in a gale. Again she began to fall behind. Ruth, noticing her friend's difficulty, halted; she kicked a stick loose from the frozen snow, picked it up and threw it for Sputnik to chase. The dog retrieved the stick and carried it dutifully back to his mistress and the game began again. Ruth and Sputnik were inseparable and went everywhere together – with the exception of school, of course. The Jack Russell terrier was a birthday present chosen by Ruth from a litter of puppies born to a bitch owned by Joshua Gregory, the village blacksmith. Ruth was eight at the time. Now aged twelve, she was the eldest of the trio by almost a year. She and Morton had lived in the village their entire lives. The pair played together at every opportunity, in and around the farm buildings, the fields, the surrounding woodlands and streams; they climbed trees together and went everywhere and anywhere where inexpensive, innocent pleasures could be enjoyed.

Abigail and her family had moved into the village from the city only eight months previously. Her mother, Mrs Markson worried constantly over her daughter's safety, fretting the instant she lost sight of her. She cringed at the thought of Abigail charging about the village in an 'unladylike manner' with Ruth and Morton and was horrified to distraction, knowing that her precious daughter would be racing down steep snow-covered slopes on a flimsy wooden sledge. Indeed, had Mrs Markson her way, Abigail would never be allowed out of the house without herself or her father as chaperone. But there, on that cold December day, liberated from parental restraint, Abigail ventured with her two friends into the dark forest.

CHAPTER 6

The wind blew colder and the sky darkened, but the three young children, distracted by their mission, remained blissfully oblivious to the changing weather. Deeper into the forest they wandered, sheltered from the turbulent and bitter wind by the rows of pine trees. Ruth teased Sputnik with a stick, she held it tantalisingly from reach before throwing it for him to chase. Her aim though was poor and the stick fell into a thicket of brambles, but the fearless dog dived in, disturbing two pheasants. The terrified birds flew up into the air, shrieking their alarm, passing low over the children's heads. Sputnik's interest in the stick became secondary, he leaped high into the air and attempted to seize hold of a pheasant, but the birds soared effortlessly from reach of the animated terrier.

The commotion on the ground excited the crows in the treetops. Cawing noisily, some hopped about the branches, steadying themselves with their wings, others circled above the trees. The crows, rooks and jackdaws were the scourge of the gamekeeper, who took pleasure from their persecution.

'I don't like it here,' said Abigail, nervously. 'I want to go home. Let's –'

'Shh!' Snapped Ruth. 'Vargis might be about.'

Abigail's anxiety increased, causing her to look sharply about in every direction. Morton remained unconcerned and watched the pheasants glide back to the earth in the distance. The birds' shrill calls echoing through the forest long after they had disappeared in the undergrowth.

Sputnik hurried back towards Ruth, looking every bit the gallant conqueror having seen off danger, dripping saliva from a pulsating pink tongue, hanging from the side of his mouth. On reaching her, the dog looked up to its mistress and whined.

'Quiet, Sputnik! We don't want Vargis finding us here. Else we'll all be for it.'

Hector Vargis was the sixty-something, tobacco-chewing gamekeeper employed by the estate to protect the game birds from predators and from poachers. He was invariably ill-tempered; feared and loathed in equal measures, admired only by the landlord because of his efficiency and dedication to his work. To those in ignorance of the nature of his profession, the gamekeeper's role seemed perverse. Once the breeding season was over and the pheasant's fattened, the shooting season began and his role changed. Instead of protector to the birds, Vargis and an army of 'sportsmen', toffs or anyone aspiring to cosy-up with the gentry, gained pleasure from blasting the birds from the sky with treasured weapons. So domesticated were the pheasants through the months of feeding and care, they had first to be terrified half-to-death by gangs carrying sticks, beating a path through the trees, whistling and yelling, urging the birds to take flight and fly in the direction of the awaiting gunmen. There, blast followed blast, as deathly showers of hot lead shot greeted the terrified pheasants. Blood and feathers rained down from the somersaulting birds, to guffaws and congratulations; 'jolly good shot, sir!'

The terror for the game birds was seasonal, but for the crows, rooks and jackdaws it was relentless and they were persecuted daily. To the hard heart of Hector Vargis the birds were vermin that might feed on pheasant's eggs, or attack the newly-hatched fledglings, and the black bird's numbers needed controlling. The gamekeeper carried his shotgun everywhere, and images of his zealous campaign littered the countryside. Birds in various stages of decay were strung up by their necks with twine and hung from tree branches and barbed-wire fences. The ghoulish ritual provided necessary proof to the landlord that the gamekeeper carried out the task for which he was paid.

'Come on, let's go,' said Ruth, striding ahead.

'But how much further is it to Blackdaw Cottage?' Abigail asked, trotting up to her. 'Is it far?'

'It's miles,' said Morton.

'Miles!' Abigail exclaimed. 'But we've walked miles already.'

'Hurry up,' urged Morton, irritably, 'or we'll never get there.'

Abigail had that day ventured further from her home than ever before, further than she might ever again be allowed if she returned home late. She felt uneasy for disobeying her mother, but the disobedience that fostered her guilt imparted a strange sensation of excitement. Excitement of the like she had never before experienced, enhanced by the thrill of venturing unaccompanied, by an adult, into the unknown. The cold, though, and periodic hunger pangs caused her to question the wisdom of the adventure and she would, if she thought she could find her way, forsake her friends and return to the comforts of home. And as for the reclusive old man that lived in the cottage in the forest, to her he looked nothing at all like the devil, as people had claimed. To Abigail, the frail, white-bearded old man reminded her of her own grandfather.

'Can't we go to Blackdaw Cottage another day?' Pleaded Abigail, through chattering teeth. 'My fingers and toes are freezing. Let's go home, Ruth. I'm cold and –'

'We're not going home,' interrupted Morton. 'We're not, are we Ruth?'

'And I'm hungry,' added Abigail, dolefully.

'You can go home if you want, but I'm not,' said Morton, firmly.

'Walk faster, and then you'll warm up,' Ruth advised her. She glanced to the darkening sky and smiling, offered her hand. 'Come on, Abigail, let's run together.'

Abigail's frown mutated into a smile. 'Oh, all right then,' she agreed, accepting Ruth's outstretched hand. She wanted to have fun but it was not easy when one's fingers and toes felt like ice. Hand in hand, the pair skipped along the snow-covered track, leaving Morton behind, kicking the snow in frustration. He summoned Sputnik to his side and played in the snow with the dog, but then realised he was being left behind.

'Wait for me!' Morton called out. 'Come on, Sputnik.'

'Hurry then,' Ruth shouted back. But she and Abigail were already out of breath and slowed down, allowing Morton to catch up.

'Anyway, why are we going to Blackdaw Cottage?' Asked Abigail. 'What's there when we get to the cottage?'

'The devil,' enthused Morton. 'We'll catch him and tie him up... Hammer a stake through his heart, like they do in films.'

'Like they do in films!' Repeated Abigail, somewhat doubtfully. 'But we can't do that.' She protested, adding disparagingly. 'And anyway that's how they kill vampires, not devils.'

Morton eyed her with contempt, affronted that a girl should possess greater knowledge of such matters than he.

'I'll set his house on fire then,' said Morton, petulantly.

Ruth and Abigail giggled, but their amusement served only to increase Morton's sense of outrage. He rummaged through a pocket and pulled out a purply-coloured wooden box.

'Look! See!' He said, shaking the box. 'I've got some matches.'

'Morton Rymer, you shouldn't carry matches,' Abigail said.

'And anyway, you wouldn't dare set Bentley's house on fire,' said Ruth.

'You'll see if I don't.'

Before another word was spoken a shotgun discharged both barrels quick-fire, stunning the trio to silence. Morton tossed the matchbox instinctively into some bushes. Sputnik barked crazily, madly.

'Sputnik!' Ruth whispered angrily, crouching low and taking hold of his collar. 'Abigail!' She implored in her next breath, grabbing the coat sleeve of her friend, dragging her earthwards behind some shrubbery. Morton was already squatted low, wide-eyed and alert, when another shot exploded, closer than before, re-igniting Sputnik's fury.

'Quiet Sputnik, quiet!' Ruth implored. Her appeal to the dog was as likely to attract the attention of the gamekeeper as was his bark, but Sputnik obeyed and stopped barking. The animal, though, remained in a heightened state of agitation and growled continually.

Several uneasy seconds passed when all that was audible was the crows' cawing, Sputnik's growl and the wind passing through the trees. When Abigail shrieked out suddenly, rising with the speed of an uncoiling spring, after a crow thudded to the ground at her feet. The snow about her was spattered crimson, and broken black feathers floated from the sky. Incensed and in hysterics, Abigail screamed out and stamped her feet.

'Shut up! Shut up, Abigail!' Urged Ruth. 'And get back down, quick!'

Abigail stood bowed, moving only her eyeballs. They

flitted from Ruth to Morton to the dead crow and back to Ruth. Then, the abrupt appearance of a black labrador, brought further muted screams. The dog halted and glanced to Abigail, before turning to Sputnik.

'Abigail!' Snapped Ruth, snatching her friend's arm, dragging her low. 'Sputnik…!'

A shrill whistle rang out, and the labrador, reminded of its task, lurched forward, seized the dead crow and trotted away with the limp bird hanging from its jaws, leaving behind a red trail on the snow.

Ruth recognised the dog. It belonged to the gamekeeper, Hector Vargis.

'Bloody fools!' A gruff voice chided from behind the crouching children. The trio turned together, looked up to the piqued figure posturing above, glaring at them, chewing fast. The shotgun, the butt tucked tight under his right arm, the barrel separated at the hinge and hanging over his forearm, seemed to validate his authority.

CHAPTER 7

The children rose up slowly under the gamekeeper's glare. Gripping the handle of a walking stick in his free hand, he jabbed it repeatedly in the snow, as his steely glare shifted from one child to the next. His jaw began to slow, and dark juices seeped from the corners of his mouth. He leaned forwards and spat.

'Ugh!' Abigail instinctively exclaimed.

The gamekeeper sniffed, dragged the arm that gripped the stick across his lips. He licked his lips and, after resuming chewing, turned to Ruth who struggled to control her straining, growling dog.

'Quieten your darned animal, can't you?' The gamekeeper barked, shifting his grip on the shotgun. 'Or I'll quieten him for you.'

'Sputnik!' Snapped Ruth, administering a sharp tug to his collar. 'Quiet, Sputnik.'

The gamekeeper cast his eyes over the children once again.

'And who gave you permission to come messing about my wood? Traipsing about... Causing mischief.' He paused, but the children remained silent. 'You should think yourselves lucky I didn't blow your blasted heads off. Forests are not playgrounds; they're dangerous places now the shooting season is underway. And there's that darned vagrant –'

'It's not your wood,' interrupted Ruth.

'Not my wood?' Repeated Vargis, exasperated.

'No, it isn't. And you can't stop us from coming here.'

'Can't I, *madam*?' The gamekeeper said, double stressing the word 'madam', chewing faster – as he was prone to do when provoked. 'Well, we'll see…' But Ruth was right, the forest was a public place and anyone was at liberty to walk its footpaths, even if it was unwise to do so during the shooting season. 'What if I'd shot one of you? What then?'

'You'd get locked up,' said Morton.

The gamekeeper laughed. 'Aye, maybe I would, but…' he turned thoughtful and rubbed his bristly chin on the back the leather-clad fist that clutched the stick. 'But what, what about Bentley? What if that old devil catches you sneaking about his home! He'd boil you and eat you.' He said, bursting immediately into laughter; unnerving laughter.

Ruth and Morton were unconcerned at his behaviour, exchanging glances and sniggering; they looked to the gamekeeper together and broke into laughter. Abigail looked on in disbelief; she detested the gamekeeper for his cruelty, but was aghast that her friends should be rude to an elder. Vargis's amusement ceased abruptly and his features hardened.

'Insolent bloody fools!' He barked, glaring at the absorbed pair, as his jaw quickened. 'What is it you two find so darned funny?' He questioned, leaning forward and spitting.

'Nothing,' replied Ruth, attempting to stifle her sniggers.

'Nothing…?'

It was the gamekeeper's dress that had triggered Ruth and Morton's laughter. Wearing an oilskin overcoat over a brown tweed jacket; a World War Two pilot's leather helmet on his head – the sheepskin-lined flaps that normally flapped loose were today buckled securely under his chin. But it was the checked olive-green knickerbockers and beige stockings he wore that had prompted the children's amusement; and when Abigail laughed, Vargis turned sharply to her, staring at her until she appeared uncomfortable. The gamekeeper's sneer then resurfaced:

'Who's this prim-looking Miss you've dragged along with you today?' Vargis questioned, pointing to Abigail with the walking stick, but looking towards Ruth.

'It's Abigail,' answered Ruth.

Abigail looked sharply to Ruth, slighted at being denied the opportunity to speak for herself.

'Abigail Markson,' emphasised Abigail, glaring at the amused gamekeeper.

'Abigail Markson!' He repeated, contemplative and shuffling. 'Newish to these parts, eh?' The gamekeeper nodded as if answering his own question, fingering his chin with a gloved forefinger. 'Aye, and I'm certain I've seen you before.' He paused. 'Aye, that's it, stepping out in the village with your mother, aye, a fine-looking woman, and I swear I've seen the likes of her before, but I'm damned if I know where.'

'Mum said gran lived in the village when she was a little girl,' Abigail informed him politely.

'Your gran lived here, did she? In this village?'

Abigail nodded: 'Yes, but it was a long time ago.'

'Yes, yes, I dare say it was,' smiled Vargis. 'Well, I'll be damned.' Exasperation caused the pitch of his voice to rise and his smile widened, as he indulged in thoughts of yesteryear, but then he remembered his purpose and his demeanour altered abruptly. He cleared his throat and shuffled. 'More blasted kids upsetting my birds.'

'It was you who upset the birds with your horrible gun, not us,' Abigail cut in, reminding the gamekeeper and surprising everyone with her outburst. She was enraged that she and her friends should be accused of causing distress to the birds when it was he who carried the shotgun, he who shot the crow that dropped dead at her feet. 'Murderer!'

'Well, well…!' Vargis said, turning and spitting. A translucent string of saliva hung from his chin, the gamekeeper drew a coat sleeve over his mouth and wiped it away. 'I'll need eyes in the back of my head… Keeping one eye on you blasted rabble, the other on that evil old devil at the cottage. There'll be no pheasants left for the guns.'

'But why do you have to shoot the pheasants?' Abigail asked, glaring.

Vargis was unprepared for such vitriol from the delicate-featured city girl; he pursed his lips and spat, before answering in a manner to match her passion.

'For sport, girl. For sport.' He was astounded that a person living in the countryside should remain ignorant of rural traditions. 'City people, huh… Know nothing of the customs of country folk, do you?' Abigail remained focused on him, but remained silent and allowed Vargis to continue. 'For sport, girl, for sport and food – delicacies for the gentry's table. To pay my wages.'

'But you don't eat crows, do you?' Abigail retaliated with renewed venom.

'Course I don't eat blasted crows,' the gamekeeper growled. 'They're vermin, like that heathen at the cottage. All should be shot.' He paused, while glaring at the children, and then his belligerent manner softened. 'Anyway it's time you lot were heading back to your homes. It'll be dark before you know it and –'

'It won't be dark yet. Not for ages,' interrupted Ruth. 'It's not even two o'clock.' She claimed, after pushing up her coat sleeve and consulting her wristwatch. 'And anyway, you can't stop us from playing in the forest.'

'Can't I now!' Vargis responded, glaring at Ruth, spitting in the snow. 'Well I'm damned if I'm shifting from this spot until you insolent lot are heading back to your homes. What have you got to say about that, *madam*?' He said, chuckling.

Ruth was at first uncertain how to respond, but she leaned close to Morton and whispered in his ear. Morton's initial bewilderment disappeared and he smiled, nodding enthusiastically.

'Come on, move!' The gamekeeper urged. 'On your way, the three of you.'

'We will,' agreed Ruth unexpectedly.

Abigail was outraged; she was freezing after standing about in the cold forest. But she detested the gamekeeper for his cruelty, for his coarseness and pleaded silently that Ruth would change her mind; disobey him.

'Come on, let's go,' Ruth said, gesticulating with a nod. She and Morton turned and strode in the direction of home. Abigail looked on in disbelief before following reluctantly, expressing her displeasure with a pronounced stomp, glaring hard at Vargis as she stepped past him. Vargis sneered victoriously.

'It's for your own darn good, young lady. And it's best you keep out of the forest... Stay clear of Blackdaw Cottage while that evil old devil lives there. Venture too close and, well...' He paused, chuckling on noticing Abigail shiver. 'Bentley'll warm you all right if he catches you... Warm the three of you in his pot.' He said, and laughed uproariously, before turning to his dog. 'Come, Jet. Time we were on our way – things to do.' The gamekeeper turned and walked away. Jet followed, still gripping the crow firmly in his jaws.

The children slowed. Turning, they observed as the gamekeeper bent and removed the crow from the Labrador's jaws. Sensing that the children had stopped, Vargis turned sharply round:

'Go on, move. Get yourselves home.' He barked. 'And keep away from Blackdaw Cottage.'

Those were the gamekeeper's final words. After straightening, he strode away, swinging the dead bird at his side by its neck, taking the luckless crow to be put on display for the benefit of his employer. Jet, relieved of his encumbrance, bounded exuberantly over in the snow. The trio, glancing intermittently over their shoulders, waited until the gamekeeper had disappeared from sight and then halted.

'Come on,' said Ruth. 'We're not taking any notice of him.' The trio doubled back and resumed their path towards the unknown, towards Blackdaw Cottage.

CHAPTER 8

All sensation of time is lost upon excitable children intent on fulfilling an adventure, and in their determination to reach the cottage the trio were blinkered to potential danger. Above them the sky grew heavier and darker, and snowflakes began to filter through the interwoven pine branches. Onwards the children progressed, unaware that in open spaces and away from the shelter provided by the pine trees, a blizzard raged. Some distance was covered at a brisk pace in relative silence, but then Morton spoke:

'I told you Bentley was the devil, and Vargis said so too... Said Bentley would murder us and –'

'Vargis never said Bentley would murder us,' interposed Ruth. 'And anyway, dad says not to believe everything Vargis says.'

'Vargis is horrid and cruel, and I bet he tells lies all the time,' Abigail added.

'You'll see if Bentley catches us,' Morton responded.

'Vargis is a stupid idiot, and you're stupid, Morton Rymer, for believing him. And anyway, tramps don't eat people.' Abigail was keen to enlighten him.

'No, but devils might!'

'Devils don't either. I know, because I've read about people eating other people and they're not devils or tramps. It's cannibals that eat other people.' Abigail informed him with an air of condescension.

'Cannibals!' Morton exclaimed. 'What, like in *Robinson Crusoe*, you mean?'

Abigail nodded. 'Cannibals only eat people when they're really hungry unless, unless they're savages as well. Savages kill people and eat them because they like to. Well, I think they do.' She turned to Ruth. 'They do, don't they, Ruth?'

Ruth shrugged. 'Expect so.'

'Savages boil people in big pots.' Abigail gestured with a sweep of her arms. 'And then they eat them all up.' She said, and burst into laughter, Ruth joining in her amusement.

'Very funny,' said Morton. 'Think you can frighten me?' He paused and turned thoughtful. 'But I wonder... Do savages take people's clothes off before they throw them in a pot and boil them?'

'Course they don't, idiot,' Abigail sounded certain. 'It'd be rude.'

'Perhaps Bentley's a savage tramp!' Suggested Morton, determined to portray the old man at the cottage a wicked person.

'No he isn't,' Ruth, interposed. 'Bentley only ever kills rabbits, that's what dad says. He says Bentley fixes a net over the rabbit's burrow, shoves a ferret down another hole, and when the rabbit runs out he catches it in the net, bashes them on their heads and kills them dead. Dad doesn't like rabbits. He says there's hundreds of the little blighters running about his fields, digging holes and dad says Bentley doesn't catch enough.'

'Does your dad like Bentley then?' Asked Abigail.

'He does when he catches lots of rabbits.'

'My dad doesn't like Bentley,' Morton said. 'My dad says the bloody old tramp should be burned alive.'

'You can't burn him alive, and you shouldn't swear, Morton Rymer,' Abigail protested. 'My dad says there's no need for swearing.'

'Well, my dad swears all the time and I'll well swear if I want to, Abigail bloody Markson.'

'Stop it this minute, or I'll tell, and then you'll be sorry.'

'It's Bentley who'll be sorry when –'

'No he won't.'

'Will when I set his house on fire… Burn the bloody old tramp alive, like dad said to.'

'Your dad's stupid,' snapped Abigail, 'and if you don't stop swearing, I'm going home.'

'Bloody go – '

'Morton Rymer, you should wash your mouth out with soap and water,' Ruth intervened. 'That's what mum tells dad when he swears. And if she could hear you now she'd never let you into our house ever again, so stop it.' Incensed and pouting, she forged on ahead, swinging her arms at her side. 'Come on, Sputnik.'

Abigail looked to Morton, smiling triumphantly, before running to catch up with Ruth. Morton hung his head and kicked the snow in frustration. After his mother left home, Morton was left in the care of an uncaring father. Mrs Evison, aware of the boy's discordant relationship with his father, had been like a second mother to him. She was there when he needed comfort or advice, she fed him, stitched his clothing and darned his socks, and was forever straightening his hair. To Mrs Evison, Morton was a respectful boy and she would have been mortified had she been witness to his language. When Morton caught up with the girls, Abigail turned to him.

'And anyway, my dad said your dad's always drunk.'

'He is,' Morton conceded, bowing his head and continuing in a barely audible mumble. 'That's why mum left. He hit her when he was drunk. Mum didn't like it. She cried and ran away and said she weren't ever coming back.'

Abigail, experiencing a pang of regret, forced a sympathetic smile. 'I'm glad my dad's not like your dad. My dad only gets drunk at Christmas. He's all right most of the time, but he locks himself in his study all day… He reckons he's writing a novel, or something and mum has to do everything, but I sometimes help.'

'I have to do everything everyday. The washing up, the shopping. I have to sweep the floor, wash all my clothes – and dad's. I wish I could live on a farm like Ruth.'

'Well, I don't know why you don't move in with us,' Ruth said. 'We've lots of rooms and mum's always feeding you anyway – washing your school things.'

'You fibber, Morton Rymer!' Retaliated Abigail, smiling. 'You said you washed *all* your own clothes!'

'Well… Not my school things.'

Dusk began to fall and the temperature plummeted, but the preoccupied children, reconciled and chatting happily, remained oblivious, or did not care. They left behind a vapour trail in their wake, like a steam train guided along iron rails to its destination. But there were no tracks in the forest to guide the three children, and the path they followed became narrower and less defined under the falling snow. Where the pine trees thinned out the path disappeared completely.

'How much further is it to Blackdaw Cottage?' Asked Abigail. 'I'm cold.'

'We're nearly there,' Ruth replied.

'I don't think I'd like to live in the forest in winter,' Morton said, shivering.

'Nor me,' agreed Ruth. 'It's much too cold in winter, but in summer it'd be fun.'

'Bentley must have a big fire in his house or he'd freeze to death,' Abigail decided.

'Mmm, I wonder what it's like inside his house?' Said Morton.

'I don't know. I've only been to Blackdaw Cottage

once. Jack took me, but we didn't go inside, and that was ages ago. Dad said to keep away.'

'Anyway, who cares what it's like in his house,' began Abigail. 'I'm not going inside. Mum wouldn't like it if I did.'

'She won't know if you don't tell her,' said Morton.

'But it's wrong to keep secrets.'

'I know lots of secrets and I don't tell them to anybody,' boasted Morton.

'Yes, you do. You tell them to me,' Ruth reminded him.

Morton looked sharply to her. 'I... Only some. I don't tell you them all.'

The children emerged into a clearing and the snow and bitter wind met them in all its arctic fury, chilling them to the bone. Snow was driven at them; it stung their cheeks and clung to their clothing, whitening them from head to foot in seconds. Blinded by the snow, the trio battled headlong into the blizzard. Only the falling snow could prevent them from reaching their intended destination. And if it did, what then for their three young lives?

CHAPTER 9

Bentley had lived at the remote cottage in the forest for much of his adult life, longer than most people could remember. Only there, in the solitude of the forest was he truly happy, surrounded by the trees, the birds and animals and his beloved white cat, Elsa. No one knew for sure whether Bentley was his first name or his surname, but no one seemed to care. Any allusions to the devil were the invention of fertile minds, or mischief from people that should know better. He troubled no one and no one troubled him, with the exception of the gamekeeper, of course. Sharing a mutual dislike and mistrust; the gamekeeper accused Bentley of poaching – catching and killing the game birds, and Bentley berated the gamekeeper for encroaching on his privacy, arriving at the cottage brandishing a shotgun, terrifying himself and his cat. The people from the village all knew that Vargis was the instigator of any disagreement, for who had not met with the gamekeeper's wrath – been accused of stealing pheasants from the estate?

The bent old man was heading home. He halted and looked about, but snow was all he could see. Snow was driven upon him by the malevolent wind; it stuck fast to his clothing, building layer upon layer and increasing his burden, and home remained some distance away. Encumbered by the weight of a bulging knapsack, Bentley resumed his journey, head-down into the blizzard, struggling and gasping, staggering through the ever-deepening snow.

The journey to the village that morning he felt had been necessary. Knowing that a prolonged and heavy snowfall might imprison him in his cottage for weeks, provisions had to be procured. Snow had been forecast to fall later that day; it had arrived earlier than expected. After purchasing provisions he should have hurried home, but the morning was bright and sunny and the temptation to linger and absorb the seasonal spirit too great. Children in the village played in the snow; they built a snowman and threw snowballs at each other – some strayed his way. He dodged them with a chuckle and threw several back. Enjoying watching the children at play had gladdened his heart, but it delayed his return. Christmas remained only weeks away, the atmosphere in the village was heady with anticipated seasonal goodwill. Children sung fragments of carols as they skipped at the sides of their mothers; mothers struggling with shopping bags swollen with presents, with treats to enhance the delights of the forthcoming festivities. Bentley, enchanted by the merry scene, rested awhile on the cold seat on the village green, absorbing the Yuletide spirit. But he lingered too long.

Up the steep slope he hauled his tiring body, puffing and panting, slipping and sliding. Thrift had made matters worse; the tread on the soles of his boots had worn thin and his feet lost grip in the snow, but worse, the thin rubber soles offered scant protection from the cold and his feet were like blocks of ice. Upwards and onwards he struggled, placing one painful foot in front of the other, knowing if he faltered he would surely perish. Exertion, the bitter weather caused his mind to wander; he thought of the days when he was young, agile and strong, before worn-out joints had become racked with arthritic pain. Then he was fit and fearless, conqueror of all terrain in all conditions, but old age had robbed him of all that.

Life in the forest had never been easy, but for Bentley the hardships had been part of the attraction when he was young; necessary to enjoy the liberty he cherished. Without freedom and open spaces, without the unpolluted forest air and the odour of the earth, without the trees and flowers, without the constancy of birdsong in his ears, the sight and sound of the forest animals, he would wither as surely would a petal detached from a flower. Blackdaw Cottage was his home, the earth and trees of the forest his lifeblood. Bentley belonged to the forest, and there, he was determined, he would remain until the end of his days.

The steep hill had at last been almost conquered and Bentley paused to catch his breath. Looking about, he noticed that swathes of snow had been disturbed, and footprints of children part-covered under the new-fallen snow – a dog's paw prints. Smiling, he shook his head and continued on his way. At the summit of the hill, he again glanced about.

'What the…!' A sledge had been abandoned by the wire-mesh fence. He looked anxiously about, expecting mischievous children to leap out, yelling to terrify him to death and pelt him with snowballs, as children from the village were apt to do. He stood and listened awhile, but all that was audible was the wind; and neither sound nor sight of children could be detected.

'Huh, kids…' Muttered Bentley, shaking his head. 'Take care of nothing these days.' He pressed on towards the iron railings that embraced the forest and there, under the overhanging branches, he found respite from the wind and relieved his back of its load. Hanging the knapsack on the iron fence, he looked back in the direction that he had travelled. In that instant the sun peeped unexpectedly through a gap in the clouds, and the falling snow thinned, granting the old man one last look upon the smoking chimneys of the village. The glare from the sun dazzled and he nipped his eyelids tight. When he reopened them, only second's later, impatient clouds had closed the fissure. The wind blew harder and colder and the snow descended thicker and faster. Bentley turned from its fury, loosening the twine that twice encircled his waist and unfastened several buttons. He pushed a hand inside his coat and removed a silver pocket watch, flicked open the case and held it at varying distances from his eyes, squinting until the Roman numerals came into sharper focus: it had turned three thirty. He compressed his lips in an expression of annoyance and snapped the watch case shut. It would be dark soon.

After replacing his treasured timepiece, he re-buttoned his coat, re-tied the twine and looked in the direction where the village had seconds earlier stood, hoping for one last look. The falling snow, though, would not grant it; and he lifted the knapsack from the railings and secured it on his back, squeezed his body through the iron-hinged kissing-gate that led into the forest.

The wind gusted hard, driving the stinging white crystals into his face. Bentley turned from it, tightening his collar and straightening his balaclava and, after adjusting his load, the stooped figure set off into the cold forest, cursing himself for loitering too long in the village. The ragged hem of his overcoat flapped angrily in the wind.

CHAPTER 10

Mrs Evison, standing at the kitchen sink, looked out through the window at the falling snow, dancing under the glow from the outside light. Sighing, she shook her head.

'It looks as though the snow's set in for the night,' she said, twisting the chromium tap. An ominous hiss and gurgling sounds followed. 'Oh, no! Whatever next?' She expressed her frustration with a pronounced sigh.

The keen frosts that had plagued the country for weeks had wrought further misery. The water supply to the farmhouse was frozen up and every drop now needed carrying from an outside source. After re-tightening the tap, Mrs Evison turned her attention to the next task from an ever-growing mental list, annoyed that neither her husband, nor either of their two children, was at hand to assist. Then the kitchen door swung suddenly open. The wind's howl heightened, and an accompanying icy blast caused Mrs Evison to shiver; she turned round swiftly.

'Where's our Ruth?' She asked, somewhat irately, the instant her bemused husband set foot inside the kitchen. Her fraught tone reflected her anxieties. 'It's high time she was back to help out.'

'Eh, what! Ruth's not home yet?' Mr Evison looked to his wife, screwing up his brow. 'Well, where…? Surely she and her friends can't be sledging still. There's work for her here… Should be here to help. Jack and me have to go back out… Bring the sheep down from the moors. If they're left until morning they'll need digging out from under the snow.'

The welfare of the animals was uppermost in Mr

Evison's mind. He and Jack had already drove the bullocks down from the pasture and had shut them inside the shed, where they would be safe and warm.

'Tell Ruth to put some hay in the rack for the bullocks when she returns.' Mr Evison said, readying himself to leave. 'Don't forget, will you?'

'No, no… I'll tell her.' His wife's tone remained strained. 'The kettle's boiling.' She said in her next breath. 'You'll have a hot drink before you leave?'

'No time… Need to go and get the sheep. It'll be dark soon.'

'Well, hold fire a minute. I'll make you a flask of hot coffee.'

'Hurry then,' he said, impatiently.

'All right, all right!' Steam was streaming from the spout of the kettle and Mrs Evison slid it from the heat. 'I do wish Ruth would hurry back though,' she said, spooning coffee and sugar into a flask, pouring in boiling water and milk. In her haste, she cross-threaded the stopper on the flask.

'Give it here,' Mr Evison said, irritably, snatching the flask from her, re-positioning the stopper and tightening it, screwing on top a plastic cup. 'Ruth can't be far away. She'll be back soon, I suppose.' He faced his wife and forced a smile.

'Yes, yes, I dare say you're right,' Mrs Evison conceded. 'But I could do with her right now to carry some water. The water pipe in the kitchen's frozen up now.'

'I'll fetch you some –'

'No, no. You go. Leave it. I'll manage until Ruth returns. You've matters more pressing to attend to than me – and I've sufficient water for now.' Glancing outside, she saw Jack walk past the window carrying a bale of hay on his back; she waved and smiled.

'Seems old Bentley's been proved right again.' Mr Evison commented, as he stepped towards the kitchen door. 'He said we'd have more snow before night – lots of it. I came across him a little over an hour ago – he was setting out for his home. I told him he'd be better off bedding down in our barn for the night. He'd be warmer than in that cold, damp cottage, I'm sure, but he'd have none of it. He'll be frozen stiff by the time he reaches that bleak place of his.'

'Aye, if he makes it home,' Mrs Evison said, turning from the window. 'Poor man. It's a wonder he doesn't freeze to death. Living in the forest in the middle of nowhere. It must be perishing – and all alone.'

The sheepdogs barking outside prompted Mr Evison to turn the door handle. 'The stubborn old fool'll live nowhere else,' he said. 'The parish council have tried to put him up in a cottage in the village, but he'll not leave his forest home. Huh, and his cat!' He stepped from the kitchen. 'Don't forget to tell Ruth to feed the bullocks, will you?'

'Yes, yes. And you take care… Take care of Jack…' Mrs Evison turned to her husband, but the kitchen door slammed shut and he was gone. Sighing, she continued with her labours.

CHAPTER 11

It was Ruth who first saw the shadowy image of Blackdaw Cottage through the falling snow. 'Look! There it is!' She called out, excited and pointing. Its gaunt form seemed almost to creep towards them through the billowy snow and the darkness, enticing the children; inviting them to enter and shelter from the storm, warm themselves in its embrace and explore its secrets.

'That, Blackdaw Cottage?' Abigail sounded decidedly unimpressed.

Indeed its impressiveness lay only in its ramshackle dereliction and the wonder was that the cottage stood at all, or that anyone would choose to live in such a desolate place. From the apex of the uneven roof, now covered in snow, protruded a crooked funnel. In places where the rust had eaten through the metal, wisps of smoke escaped, which was swiftly smothered under the falling snow. The window frames were uneven and the walls either bulged outwards or caved inwards, and the mortar that bonded the stones together bore patches of plaster of different shades, evidence that a much restorative work had been carried out over the years. In fact, every feature of the cottage was deficient in one way or another. Left of the building stood a rickety wooden shed; around it snow was forced at great speed by the wind.

High up in the trees and blotted from view by the falling snow, squabbling crows cawed noisily. The birds perhaps fought with each other in an attempt to secure the best-sheltered spot in old nests – if shelter could be found at such altitude in the grip of a blizzard. But maybe the presence of humans made the birds nervous, recalling previous encounters with the over-zealous gamekeeper.

Abigail shivered: 'Shall we go home now?'

'Go home!' Exclaimed Morton, in disbelief. 'We've only just got here.'

'Best wait… See if it stops snowing,' Ruth advised, turning and facing the cottage. 'We should see if we can get inside… Shelter from the snow a while.'

Morton led the way, but as he was almost upon the door of the cottage the wind gusted, generating an eerie howl that stopped him stopped in his tracks.

'It's only the wind,' decided Ruth, smiling and bustling past him. 'Come on.'

'I'm glad I don't live here,' uttered Abigail, through chattering teeth, keeping close to Ruth. 'It's much too scary.'

A snowball whizzed inches past Ruth's ear and splattered against the house wall. She turned instinctively.

'Idiot!'

Morton, grinning, crouched and gathered more snow. He straightened and readied himself to release a second snowball.

'Don't you dare, Morton Rymer!'

Morton thought better of it and allowed the snow to slip through his fingers to the ground. He caught up with the two girls, and Ruth was about to knock on the cottage door when they found themselves surrounded by noisy jackdaws, agitated and cawing. Abigail's screams excited the birds further, as did Sputnik's bark.

'Let's go home,' pleaded Abigail, holding her head in her hands, looking with dread to the frenetic birds.

The snow fell thick and fast, the wind blew harder, and it seemed as if nature's forces conspired in order to force the children into the cottage, urging them to choose the sensible option and shelter from the storm.

'We can't go home yet,' Ruth said, blinking the snow from her eyes. 'Not until it stops snowing. Best see if we can open the door.'

'But won't Bentley be in?' Questioned Abigail.

'He can't be,' Morton spoke with certainty. 'I saw him in the village this morning and if he'd got back we'd have seen him. And anyway, I'm not scared of Bentley.'

'You knock on the door then,' said Ruth.

'I will,' Morton replied, stepping boldly up to it and knocking. Standing there transfixed, as if he expected the door to fly open, to come face to face with the devil. The door, though, remained closed.

'Let's go home,' Abigail again pleaded. 'I want to go home. I'm cold and I'm hungry.'

The three young adventurers were each cold and hungry, but visibility under the falling snow was reduced to mere yards, and home and a nourishing hot meal in front of a blazing fire remained an unreachable aspiration. Danger lurked with every false step. The forest was vast and under the darkness and swirling snow; one area was indistinguishable from the next. Blackdaw Cottage offered the children the only place of refuge: they must enter and secure shelter or they would surely freeze.

Ruth lifted up the latch and pushed hard and the door creaked open. Sputnik, impatient and whining, squeezed inside the instant he was able, disappearing in the murkiness. Ruth followed.

'Hello!' She called out, angling her head and listening. All that was audible was the pitter-patter of Sputnik's feet on the stone floor, and worrying scratching in the rafters. Tentatively, she stepped deeper into the dark room, trembling from the cold and from fear.

'Is anyone in there?' Morton called to her, from the safety of the doorway.

Ruth ignored him and called again. 'Hello! Anybody home?' This time, she spoke with conviction, before turning to her two friends. 'Come on,' she urged, beckoning them with an eager wave. Morton and Abigail stepped over the threshold and joined her in the unlit room, leaving the door purposely ajar in order to allow in what little light remained.

As the children's eyes adjusted to the darkness, objects became clearer. To their amazement the trio discovered that the interior of Blackdaw Cottage was much like any other home. Against a wall stood a cupboard. There were chairs and a table and shelves stacked with pots and pans. There was even a sink! But most comforting of all was the homely smell of a wood fire burning.

'And the fire's alight,' enthused Ruth, hastening towards it after noticing smoke rising from beneath the grey ash. 'We'll be all right here.'

Abigail remained unconvinced. 'But why can't we go home? You know the way, don't you, Ruth?'

'She would if she could see where she was going,' Morton intervened. 'And so would I.'

'Where's the light switch?' Abigail next asked, searching about. 'It's dark and –'

'The light switch?' Repeated Morton, somewhat incredulously.

'There's no electricity in here,' said Ruth, pointing to a lamp that was suspended from a wire hook attached to the rafters. 'Look. That's what Bentley uses to see in the dark – an oil lamp.'

'An oil lamp!'

'Everybody had oil lamps before electricity was invented,' Ruth informed her. 'Didn't you know?'

Abigail remained tight-lipped, unwilling to expose the gap in her knowledge.

'Where's Sputnik?' Wondered Morton, turning one way and then the other, when a tin can fell to the floor and rolled disconcertingly over the stone flags. Sputnik's bark erupted with unbridled fervour amid scuffling and scurrying and heightened scratching in the rafters. Dust and feathers fell upon the motionless children standing open-mouthed and looking to each other through widening eyes, shuffling instinctively closer together. Together they gasped and screamed their terror.

CHAPTER 12

The falling snow, its rapid progression into a raging blizzard instilled an acute sense of urgency to all that remained exposed to its wrath. Danger, even death, awaited those who disregarded its power, or those that misjudged their journey and found themselves caught up in its fury.

Vargis was aware of the dangers and today he worked with immediacy at odds with his normal indolent manner. He and his dog, Jet, had descended from the higher reaches of the forest and was within a short distance of the fields that led to the road and to the village. His work was almost done, and in the diminishing light he hurried towards a rusted metal barrel, grunting his annoyance at the snow blowing upon him.

After propping his gun and stick against the barrel, he lifted off the heavy metal lid. Grain was stored inside, which was used to supplement the pheasant's natural diet of insects, worms and grubs, during the winter months. The gamekeeper, after setting the lid down, reached inside the barrel, picked up the bucket that lay on the grain, and scooped corn into it. Whistling – a sound that the pheasants were familiar with – he stepped from the barrel, spilling corn from the leaking bucket. Elaborately-coloured birds ran after him from every direction, flapping their wings to gain extra speed, following the trail of corn he threw down to them. The pheasants seemed to share the gamekeeper's urgency and pecked greedily at the corn, some birds, in their eagerness, passed between his legs, almost tripping him up.

'Blasted greedy birds! Get out of it,' he ranted, throwing

a handful of grain over them. When the bucket was empty, Vargis, chewing slowly, stood admiring the vibrant birds as they filled their crops – an internal pouch in which food is stored for digesting later – with the corn. A violent gust reminded him of the need to hurry, and he tossed the bucket inside the barrel, bent and lifted the lid up from the ground. Groaning and grimacing, he struggled with it against the might of the wind. Snow was blown into his eyes and made them water.

'Blasted snow!' He growled, blinking repeatedly, slamming the lid down on top of the barrel, leaving it askew, as he turned and spat. Misjudging the direction of the wind, his spittle was blown back into his face.

'Blasted wind!' He roared, wiping a sleeve over his face. Jet, interpreting his master's rant as a cue for play, frolicked at his side. 'Down! Get out of it, blasted stupid hound.' Whilst distracted, the wind seized its chance and snatched the lid from the gamekeeper's grasp. It landed on its rim and was driven from him over the frozen snow. 'Come blasted back! Damn it!' He yelled, chasing after the lid, running awkwardly over the snow. Jet raced alongside him, barking. 'Quiet…! Daft bloody sod.' He yelled, kicking snow over the excitable animal and almost losing his footing.

The gamekeeper caught up with the lid only after it had collided with a tree and toppled over. Chewing fast, breathing heavily, he bent and lifted the lid up from the ground. Jet, standing close by, shook snow from his coat over him.

'Damn it! Sod off, dog or I'll, I'll…' He yelled, threatening the animal with the lid, but Jet still in playful mode, barked and raced about in the snow.

Vargis carried the lid back to the barrel and, after scooping out the wet corn with a hand, he secured it with two large boulders he found beneath the snow. 'There! Let's see you blow that off!' He said, with a defiant chuckle; looking about as though the wind could see him, and he could see the wind. After pulling his collar tight about his neck, he picked up his shotgun and stick and set out for home. The blizzard worsened and darkness fell early, but the gamekeeper, having tramped the route many times before, could have found his way home with both eyes closed.

In all the years that Vargis had lived in the countryside, never had he witnessed a blizzard to match the ferocity and persistency of the present storm. Snow fell relentlessly, hour after hour. Snow was lifted from the ground by the wind and driven into deepening drifts, piling high around walls, hedges and fences; it was indiscriminate, smothering everything and everyone.

The gamekeeper hurried home along the road. His fingers and toes were devoid of all feeling, and he cursed himself for setting out that morning wearing knickerbockers and boots, but he had not expected the blizzard to blow up as fast and with such ferocity. No one had.

Through the roar of the wind he detected the muffled clang of the blacksmith's hammer striking metal. Joshua Gregory's furnace would be alight. His smile widened and his step quickened.

There was little possibility of quickening footsteps high up on the moors though. Mr Evison, Jack and their trusted sheepdogs battled against the driving snow, trying their utmost to keep the bleating sheep on the correct path for home. The animal's thin legs sunk easily into the soft snow and at times the bemused animals struggled to move at all. Progress was slow, painfully so, and there was always one rebellious animal that refused to conform to perceived wisdom, taking a chance and breaking away from the flock. The sheepdogs, though, were alert; springing speedily into action and rounding up any animal that strayed, bringing them quickly back into line.

The thick falling snow was disorientating; and in the confusion, exacerbated by the intense cold, it was at times impossible to determine the direction of the farm. Instinct alone could not be relied upon, but clues remained visible to those who were familiar with the layout of the land. The fall of a gully, strategically placed boulders of different sizes – covered in snow but recognisable – were scattered about the land, a gap in a wall, or an anaemic hawthorn bush reassured father and son they were headed in the right direction. The ruddy-faced men though were frozen, numbed from head to foot by the cold, and it would be some time yet before the pair could relax in the warmth and safety of the farmhouse.

CHAPTER 13

The doors of the blacksmith's workshop were thrown wide open; they always were whatever the weather when Mr Gregory was busy at work. Jet entered first, shaking the snow from his coat and wagging his tail in anticipation of a cordial welcome.

'All I blasted need!' The blacksmith grumbled, halting and looking to the bedraggled dog, knowing that Vargis would be close behind. He put down the hammer, pushed the goggles up onto his forehead and raised the horseshoe that he gripped between a pair of tongs level with his eyes. After examining it from every angle, he set the horseshoe back down on the anvil, lowered the goggles over his eyes and picked up the heavy hammer and continued with his work. Sparks and smoking chaff flew from the metal. Jet, shuffling slowly closer, looked up to the industrious blacksmith, and then sniffed his legs.

'Get out of it, hound!' Snarled the blacksmith, kicking out. The movement and noise from the brown leather apron, reaching almost to the floor, was sufficient to send Jet scurrying back. 'Get yourself burned... Get me into bother with...' The blacksmith glanced outside to the approaching whitened figure and scowled. Jet sauntered forlornly away and sat on the warm stone flags by the forge, licking his wet coat.

'Foul afternoon,' Vargis complained as he entered, unbuckling his leather hat. 'Fit for neither man nor beast.'

'Thought you was a beast... Abominable snowman.' Laughed the blacksmith.

'Abominable bloody weather... Blasted clown,' Vargis retaliated, taking his shotgun and walking stick into the same hand, wiping the snow from his brow with his other hand.

The blacksmith glanced at the gamekeeper. 'Abominable… Aye.' He grinned and continued with his work.

Vargis backed away, wincing each time the hammer struck the metal. After setting his gun and stick down on a bench, the gamekeeper pulled the gloves from his hands and removed his hat, spreading the wet garments on a ledge by the furnace to dry. He warmed his hand and fingers in the glow from the furnace, and returned to the blacksmith.

The metal that the industrious man worked was cooling and extra effort was needed to rend it into the required shape. Vargis, standing watching, pulled a rusted tin from out of a coat pocket and prised off the lid. With a forefinger and thumb he pinched out a wad of tobacco, pushed it into his mouth and chewed. The hammering stopped.

'Terrible weather,' said Vargis.

'Is it?' The blacksmith replied sardonically, lifting the goggles up onto his forehead, inspecting the horseshoe once more time. 'What of it?' He added in the same tone. But before the gamekeeper had the opportunity to respond, the horseshoe was set back down on the anvil and struck four, five, six more times. Mr Gregory then checked his artwork one more time, and tossed the finished product into a tub of murky water. The metal hissed as it disappeared; bubbles formed on the surface and floated fleetingly before expiring.

Joshua, straightening, grimaced. He turned to Vargis, smudging the beads of sweat on his brow with the back of a hand.

'I'll be surprised if anyone can get into the village,' the gamekeeper remarked.

'Why would anyone want to?' Replied the blacksmith, stepping past him, the leather apron flapping about his legs. He took a rectangular metal strip from a pile, carried it to the furnace and thrust it under the hot coals, burying it from sight with the tongs.

'Bloody work…' the blacksmith complained, turning back to Vargis, wiping his brow once again. 'No end to it.'

'Well, if you're busy, you're earning,' said Vargis. 'Man cannot survive without money.'

'Aye, I dare say you're right,' the blacksmith agreed, stroking his moustache with a forefinger and thumb. 'It's all right for some, though, those with nothing to do other than stroll about the countryside all day.'

The gamekeeper, nodding distractedly, quickened his jaw suddenly and shot an angry glare at the blacksmith. 'I hope you're not referring to me?' He growled, leaning forward and spitting on the floor. The blacksmith looked on with disgust, but a sneer stretched his whisker-obscured lips.

'And what if I was?' He asked. 'You do sod all else except traipse about all day in those silly trousers – in this weather, I ask you, spitting for all England and you've the gall to call it work.' The blacksmith laughed, but a cough curtailed his amusement. 'Bloody dust… Gets everywhere… Your eyes, your nose, your throat, your bloody arsehole, I shouldn't wonder. But it wasn't you I was referring to… It's him at the cottage I meant. He you fools mollycoddle.'

'What!' Roared Vargis, chewing fast. 'Me mollycoddle that blasted peasant, that pheasant thief! I'd mollycoddle him all right if I had my way –'

'But surely he could be put to some use?'

'Put to some use! Put down, more like!' Snapped Vargis, his jaw quickening and his face flushing. 'The good for nothing... Stealing my birds. I'd mollycoddle him all right, aye, with lead shot.'

The blacksmith shook his head and laughed. 'Then why doesn't the forestry people kick him out of the cottage if he's trouble? It's their forest, their property.'

'Live and let live. That's what those fools say. I've told them there'd be more birds for the guns with that old rogue out of the way. Huh, they'll not listen to me – might as well talk to the shithouse wall – and as for the law, well what–'

'The law?' Interrupted the blacksmith. 'What can the law do? Bentley's committed no crime.' He said, as he poked about the hot coals with the tongs, finding the rectangle he had buried earlier, gripping it between the tongs and drawing it out. The sparkling metal glowed red, but the blacksmith reburied it; he swung round and faced Vargis. 'The old man's harmless.'

'Harmless!' Vargis barked, brown juices glistening at the corners of his mouth. 'Harmless!' He repeated, wiping his mouth on the back of a hand. 'That heathen, that filthy old devil'll bring a plague to finish us all. It's happened before.'

The blacksmith shook his head and laughed. 'Times have changed,' he said, pointing with the tongs to the gamekeeper's legs, 'but anyone coming across you might not think so.' Coughing again halted the blacksmith's laughter.

'Choke... Sarcastic blasted goat,' said Vargis, eyeing the blacksmith irefully. 'I'm telling you, that old devil at the cottage is nothing but trouble.'

'An eyesore, maybe... Wandering about the village in rags, but he's harmless. I'd swear on my wife's life.'

'You haven't a wife.'

Joshua, opening and closing the tongs, smirked. 'No,

but had I a wife, I'd swear Bentley was nothing more than a lonely old man. Useless maybe, but harmless.'

'Nothing would give me greater pleasure than empty a cartridge of lead shot between his eyes.' Vargis said.

'You're all talk, Hector. You know you don't mean it.'

'I do mean it! Damn it, I do!'

'Have you no grain of compassion? Old Bentley's had a hard time recently. Living in that cold, damp place in the middle of the worst winter in decades.'

'And whose fault's that? No one forces him to live in a ruin in the middle of a forest. Let him freeze, I say. Humph, no point getting sentimental over the stubborn fool.'

'Well, I suppose he's a right to live where he chooses, like anyone else.'

'Right!' Vargis had worked himself up into a frenzy. 'What rights have vermin? Shoot him, I say. Poison him, but be rid.' His jaw worked fast and furious, and then he leaned forward and spat on the floor at the feet of the blacksmith.

The blacksmith looked down; he looked up slowly and faced the gamekeeper. 'I'd thank you for not spitting that filth all over my floor.'

'Uh!' Vargis uttered, scuffing a boot over the wet patch, looking meekly up to the sturdy blacksmith.

'Bentley's been around for years. What harm's he done you?'

'What about my pheasants?'

'What about your bloody pheasants!' Mocked the blacksmith. 'The poor buggers get shot anyway… Huh, by a bunch of strutting buffoons, gentrified clowns with more money than sense.'

Vargis compressed his lips in outrage, and watched the blacksmith retrieve the now white-hot metal in the jaws of the tongs and carry it to the anvil, where he began rending the metal into the required shape.

'Never hear you complain when I drop you a brace of pheasants.' Vargis said, shuffling closer.

Joshua halted the hammer shoulder-high and looked to the gamekeeper. 'The peasants are already dead, what's the point?' The hammer slammed down onto the metal and Vargis lurched back when hot sparks shot his way. He turned and walked to the forge, recovered his hat and put it on his head, leaving the straps dangling. He picked up his gloves and, pulling them on, he stepped to the bench.

'Everyone's gone soft,' Vargis uttered, picking up his shotgun and walking stick, tucking the gun under his arm. He stood a while observing the blacksmith, marvelling at the ease and swiftness the familiar horseshoe began to take shape. The gamekeeper then shuffled towards the open door and looked outside. Snow fell relentlessly in the darkness, where and all sound seemed strangely muffled. Only the rhythmical hammer rang true, sounding like church bells summoning mourners to a funeral.

Vargis turned and whistled. Jet raised his head and looked to his master, but appeared reluctant to move. 'Jet!' The gamekeeper snapped irritably, stepping outside. Jet jumped up and raced to his master. 'I'll bid you good day, Joshua.' He said, turning to the blacksmith.

Joshua halted the hammer mid-flight. 'Aye, and mind how you go… Ouch!' The blacksmith dropped the hammer, the tongs and the horseshoe. 'Damn and blast!' He yelled out, shaking his left hand, jumping about. Vargis, grinning, turned round; he turned back and then he and Jet disappeared into the blizzard and the darkness.

CHAPTER 14

Mrs Markson turned from the irritating ticking clock. It had turned five o'clock and Abigail had still not returned home. Shaking her head and sighing, she stepped to the lounge window, pushed the curtain aside and looked outside, squinting hard into the billowy snow and hoping that she might see the image of her daughter approaching.

'Where on earth can she be?' She uttered despairingly, turning back to the clock and re-checking the time. It was five minutes past five exactly. Never before had Abigail been more than a few minutes late home for tea, and she had promised faithfully to return home by four o'clock at the latest.

Mrs Markson pressed her face to the glass pane and looked left and right. She looked hard in every direction, willing her daughter to appear and appease her fears. Wringing her wrists, stroking her face and fingering her hair, scratching her head, she stepped from the window and began pacing the room.

'Those two ragamuffins leading Abigail astray. I should never have listened to Clive. Should never have let her go sledging with those two... Oh-h-h...' Her heart clung to hope but her head alerted her to the possibility that something was wrong, terribly wrong. She knew how Abigail despised the cold; those awful winds that made her ears ache and her forehead throb. Her daughter, Mrs Markson knew, would chose the luxury of home and a book before a warm fire, to boisterous play outdoors in the cold fields in the snow. And it was hours since she left home with her friends, Ruth and Morton; Abigail would be frozen half to death.

'My poor, darling! How will ever she survive?' She spoke out loud, opening the curtain and looking in horror at the snow being driven against the windowpanes, as if to amplify the dangers. She let go of the curtain, gripped a clump of hair and twisted it around her fingers until it hurt. 'Why, oh why, did I listen to Clive? If only I'd been more assertive. If only the snow would stop! If the wind didn't blow! If… Oh, if, if!'

This was the Markson's family's first experience of winter in the remote rural village and right now Mrs Markson hoped that it would be their last. Snowstorms, like the one ravaging the country right now, had not been factored into their calculations when they decided to leave behind the perils of the city. During inclement weather in the city, shelter was never far away, but where could shelter be found in the middle of a field? Thoughts that Mrs Markson could hardly dare think started to trouble her. Perhaps Abigail and her friends had met with an accident! Perhaps they had been buried alive under the snow! Perhaps…! The longer her daughter remained absent, the more anxious she became. She stepped to the door, gripped the doorknob and was about to turn it, but she checked herself.

'No, no, I mustn't.'

But Mrs Markson hesitated for only a moment further, before summoning the courage to turn the doorknob and open the door. She set off at great speed towards the library and burst in without knocking.

Clive, her husband, turned: 'What the…!'

'Abigail has still not returned,' she blurted out quickly. 'What are we to do, Clive?'

'Nothing, woman! Nothing!' He swivelled round in his chair and glared. 'For goodness sake, woman, get a grip of yourself…'

'But…!' Mrs Markson stared back in disbelief.

Clive had supposedly been engrossed in his work – he claimed to be writing a novel. Adhering diligently to the same routine each day; shutting himself in the small library at eight-thirty precisely each morning, day after day, week after week, month after month. Click, click, day in, day out. Neither Mrs Markson nor Abigail had seen a chapter, a paragraph, or a single sentence from his hours of secluded labour. The only evidence of Mr Markson's industry was the monotonous sound of the typewriter keys, which could be heard throughout the house, every few seconds click, click. No one was allowed to enter the library unless Mr Markson was present, and when he was away from home he locked the door and took the key; such was his obsession for secrecy.

'How many times do I have to I tell you not to disturb me when I'm busy – ruining my concentration? You know how I detest being disturbed.'

'Yes, yes, Clive but –'

'But what, woman? Why do you do it?'

Perhaps there was no book at all! Thought Mrs Markson. That was it! That was why he was angry. He was embarrassed.

'How can I concentrate when I'm interrupted constantly over nothing at all?'

'Nothing!' Repeated his wife, enraged. 'Abigail… Nothing! Have you not seen…?'

'Of course I've seen the flurry of snow. Think I'm blind, woman? One expects snow showers in the middle of winter in the middle of the countryside. It'll stop in five minutes, you'll see. Now go… Leave me to my work.'

Mrs Markson was incensed. 'I knew it was a bad idea. I should never have listened to, to –'

'That's right, blame me. Blame me like you always do.'

'But why! Why did you interfere...? Give Abigail permission to go sledging with those two ragamuffins, after I...' She took a deep breath and calmed her anger.

'Kids love playing out in the snow. They get carried away... Become neglectful of the time.' Mr Markson's tone was softer and he swivelled back round in his chair. Click, click.

Mrs Markson remained furious though; she clenched her fists and tugged her hair and then stomped towards the door. She turned and said, 'why we ever decided to come to this village in the first place, miles from anywhere, I honestly don't know!'

'Your idea, I believe,' interrupted Mr Markson, with a mischievous chuckle.

'If that filthy old tramp gets hold of Abigail who knows what might happen.' She blurted. 'Perhaps she's been kidnapped already!'

'What, the three of them?' Mr Markson faced his wife, he pointed to the typewriter on the desk in front of him. 'It's you that should be writing this, not me. Your imagination is more fertile than mine.' He turned from her. 'If you must talk nonsense, go into the lounge and talk to yourself. How can I concentrate, forced to listen to your hysterics? The children will be at the Evison girl's farm. Go phone them, go put your mind at ease, but leave me to my writing. And don't disturb me again over trivial matters.'

'Trivial matters!' Mrs Evison shook with rage. She yanked open the library door and turned. 'Our daughter's safety's no trivial matter, I can tell you.' She yelled, before storming from the room, slamming the door behind her with every ounce of strength she could muster. Clive almost jumped out of his seat.

'Blasted woman!' He snapped, yanking a sheet of paper

from the typewriter, screwing it into a ball and throwing it onto a growing pile on the floor. He put another sheet of paper into the typewriter and typed a few more words before abandoning his work. Sighing and reclining in his chair, he cupped the back of his head in his hands and stared outside through the small, high window. With widening eyes, he rose, stepped slowly to the window and looked outside; he gasped.

Mrs Markson, standing in the draughty hall with the telephone receiver held to her ear, straightened the crocheted mat on which the telephone set sat with her free hand. She exhaled with frustration, grimaced and slammed the receiver back into its cradle.

'Clive'll be right... Always is.' She uttered angrily, hurrying from the hall and into the lounge. She closed the door and stepped to the window where she stared outside, disconsolate, watching the snow, listening to the wind when the lounge door opened.

'Why didn't you tell me? Make me understand!' Mr Markson said. Seated at his typewriter, immersed in a fantasy world, he was removed from reality and had failed to grasp the severity of the situation facing them, and had been oblivious of the ferocity of the blizzard.

CHAPTER 15

As unexpected lightning strikes fear into the hearts of the bravest, the white cat, meowing as if mortally wounded, sent the children's heart rate soaring as it sprang out of the gloom and raced outside with Sputnik just inches from its tail.

'Sputnik!' Yelled Ruth, breathing heavily, breaking into a smile of relief.

Fear all abated once the children realised that their moment of terror was borne of nothing more sinister than a cat. Sputnik halted abruptly, he skidded on the stone floor and went tumbling head over tail outside into the snow. After scrambling to his feet, the animal returned to his mistress panting and wagging his tail, looking every bit the gallant protector having seen off danger. Ruth bent and stroked him:

'Ugh... You wet brave thing!' She said.

The door was closed and the snow and malevolent wind shut out, along with Bentley's cat. The children removed their wet garments and, as children are apt to do with little thought, the coats and gloves, scarves and hats were thrown on a heap onto a chair. Ruth, glancing about, detected wisps of white smoke rising up through the ashes in the grate. She picked up a poker and, after riddling away the ash, uncovered glowing cinders, on to which she arranged several logs from the stack on the hearth.

The fireplace and built-in cooking range was set into the lime-washed wall that divided the cottage into two. The appliance, or similar models, were fixtures in homes throughout the land before the invention of gas and electric cookers. Two cast-iron doors were set on each side of the fire, where Bentley cooked his food. A metal arm with a hook on the end could receive either a kettle or a cooking pot, and provided an additional facility to the ovens.

Abigail remained nervous and looked constantly towards the door, fearing that Bentley might return and rebuke them for trespassing on his property. Morton, though, harboured no such fears and was busy carrying chairs to the fireside, arranging them in an arc around the fire. The job done, he sat, pulled off his boots and invited the girls to join him. After removing their boots the trio sat in silence, warming their toes and wondering perhaps when they might next be reunited with their families, when a whistle that pitched higher and louder caused them to look anxiously to each other. With widening eyes they listened to the wind screech to a climax, only to begin all over again. The children smiled and relaxed. Sputnik, looking to Ruth and whining, meandered closer. She leant forward in her seat and stroked her dog's head.

'I wonder if dad and Jack have got the sheep down from the moors yet, the bullocks into the shed?'

'Bullocks! What's a bullock?' Asked Abigail.

'A bull with its bollocks chopped off,' replied Ruth with honest abruptness.

'Is it?' Responded Abigail, puzzled and frowning.

'Well, that's what Jack told me.'

Abigail remained thoughtful. 'What's a bollock?' She next asked, looking to Ruth, but it was Morton who spoke.

'Those round dangly things boy-things have,' he informed her, eager to impress upon her his knowledge of such matters.

'Oh…' Abigail uttered with indifference, compressing her lips and turning her attention to her toes, rubbing them vigorously before slipping her feet back into the warmed wellington boots. She remained uneasy still and looked periodically towards the door. But the weather remained hostile and it was unlikely that Bentley, or anyone else, would be able to find their way to the cottage through the blizzard.

Morton put his boots back on and stood. After looking briefly about he was drawn to the white enamelled sink glinting under the light from the fire. The sink was set against the wall opposite the entrance and a tap, fixed to the end of a pipe, protruded halfway over it. Curiosity got the better of Morton and he strode up to it, grasped hold of the tap and opened it. To his amazement water flowed from it.

'Look, see!' He said, turning to the two girls.

From where the water flowed was anyone's guess. The cottage was not connected to the mains, and much of the supply of water to the village had been frozen up now for some days, forcing the residents to collect water where they could find it. Some hacked through the ice on the river, scooping water out in buckets; others collected snow and melted it in saucepans. Morton turned off the tap and returned to his friends at the fireside. The trio succumbed to silence and sat watching the flames while their bodies absorbed the warmth from the fire, pondering over their predicament.

In their quest for adventure the children had failed to comprehend the level of distress their adventure would impact upon the minds of their parents. But childhood is bliss and danger seems somehow less threatening. The children felt safe, and Blackdaw Cottage was surprisingly cosy, furnished as any home in the village might be. Right of the sink, several shelves were fixed to a wall; the place Bentley stored his pots and pans and plates. Left of the entrance, between the door and a window, stood a large cupboard. The lower section contained two columns of drawers of varying sizes, three deep, the largest at the bottom and the smallest at the top. The upper portion served as a display unit. On either side of a cracked mirror were two slim rectangular glass doors. Behind, shelves were crammed with decorated plates, bone china cups and saucers, pewter goblets and porcelain cats. A collection of toby jugs (beer mugs or ornamental jugs bearing faces of old men wearing three-cornered hats) with faces that would frighten the life from anyone encountering similar life forms on a dark night. On the wall opposite, between the sink and another window, stood a cabinet with more drawers; on top was a half-emptied bottle of whisky. Nearby, a rectangular wooden table was positioned by the window; perfectly positioned to take advantage of the light – if the hessian curtains were ever opened. Pushed under two sides of the table were four chairs with fraying wicker seats. All had at some time been hauled the long distance from the village.

'What if Bentley comes back?' Asked Abigail, nervously.

'I'll bash him with… With…' began Morton, looking about.

'With nothing,' Ruth intervened, observing his fruitless search.

'You'll see,' said Morton, searching still. 'I'll fight him with the poker.'

'Anyway, he won't come back tonight, not now,' Ruth said confidently. 'No one would be able to find their way through the snow, not even Bentley.'

'But we'll be able to find our way home won't we, Ruth?' Abigail asked.

Ruth shrugged. 'Don't think so, not tonight.'

Indeed, darkness had been with them for some time, and the blizzard blew still. But even if it was to cease at that moment there was little possibility of anyone leaving the cottage that night. The wind whipped the icy crystals up from the ground to meet the falling snow, swirling it into a blinding fog; and anyone foolish enough to step into its cauldron would be consumed within minutes, condemned to perish within its icy wrath for their folly.

Morton noticed the crude wooden bowl at the centre of the table – carved perhaps by Bentley – and his eyes widened. The bowl was piled high with fruits of every kind; apples and pears, bananas with speckled black skins, tangerines and purple grapes.

'I'm hungry,' said Morton, standing and stepping towards the table. The girls' eyes followed him. 'There's peanuts as well!' He declared, thrusting a hand into the bowl and withdrawing it filled with beige-coloured pods. 'Look! See!'

Ruth dragged a small table between the chairs and the fire. 'Fetch the bowl here.'

'But we can't eat Bentley's food,' protested Abigail. 'It's stealing.'

'Who cares,' said Morton, picking up the fruit bowl. 'I'm starving.'

'Better to steal than starve to death,' Ruth said. 'And we can't ask Bentley if he's not here, can we?'

Morton passed Ruth the bowl and, after setting it down on the table, she quickly selected the biggest peanut she could find and cracked the shell open. She removed the nuts and stuffed them into her mouth and chewed. Morton, after sitting, did likewise, but Abigail, her stomach rumbling, sat watching the pair enjoying the peanuts.

'Get some, Abigail,' urged Ruth, sliding the bowl nearer her. 'Bentley won't mind, and if he does dad'll pay.' She said, picking up a tangerine, peeling it and tossing the skin onto the fire. The orange peel, after lying on the flames only seconds, ignited with a fizz, spouting blue and orange flame. Abigail turned from the spectacle to Ruth and watched as her friend split the tangerine in two and peel off a segment. 'Want one?' Ruth said, attempting to tempt Abigail with the fragrant juicy fruit.

Abigail shook her head, but she smiled and selected a tangerine from the bowl for herself and began peeling it. Morton discovered that the black-skinned bananas were sweet and not at all as unappetising as they might have appeared, but after walking in the cold for miles, being without food the entire time, he would have eaten almost anything.

The three children feasted on the fruits and nuts until the bowl was empty and sat basking in the glow from the fire, content with filled stomachs. After a while, Abigail's eyes were drawn to the two framed sepia photographs that hung on the wall, one at each side of the fireplace. They were portraits of a smiling handsome face, a man, and in the piercing stare that looked back she sensed a profound familiarity, as if she had been acquainted with the image all her life. She rose from her chair and studied the portraits at close range, the one to her right first: a young man in his twenties, she guessed. She stepped across the hearth to the second photograph. It was the same man, but the photograph was obviously taken later in life. Abigail scrutinised the pictures long and hard, stepping from one to the other, before returning to her seat, deep in thought, certain that she had encountered the same abstracted gaze somewhere before.

'Bentley looked quite handsome when he was young, don't you think?' Abigail said.

'Handsome!' The tone of Morton's exclamation suggested he disagreed.

'Mm… Maybe,' murmured Ruth, standing and

glancing at the photographs on passing. She continued to the window, Sputnik scampering after her, and drew the hessian curtain aside and attempted to look outside, but snow had built up over the windows and obscured her view.

'It's never going to stop snowing, is it, Ruth?' Asked Abigail, glumly.

'Doesn't look like it, not yet,' replied Ruth, even though she could see little or nothing at all of the outside world. She let go of the curtain, bent and fussed over her dog. After straightening, she set off at a trot. 'Come, Sputnik, let's see what's in the other room, shall we?'

'Wait for me!' Morton called out, rising hurriedly from his chair and racing after them.

The room was dark and gloomy, and Ruth draped the curtain over a chair to allow in what little light was available. Meanwhile, Sputnik scurried about the room with his nose to the floor with the keenness of a bloodhound on discovering an interesting scent. A large bed occupied much of the room. Its headboard was pushed tight against the dividing wall where the bricks, after absorbing the heat from the fire throughout the day, would help to keep the bed aired. Covering the bed was a generous-sized patchwork quilt, large enough to cover a bed twice its size; its bulk indicated that it would be warm. A pair of matching chests, positioned on each side of a wardrobe, was set against the wall at the foot of the bed. An upended orange box, divided equally by a single piece of wood, sufficed as a bedside cabinet. On its shelf were a clock, a comb and several items personal to Bentley. At the far side of the bed on a chair, matching the one supporting the curtain, was a crimson cushion with a hollowed centre. With the exception of electrical appliances and a supply of electricity, Bentley's cottage was little different from any home in the village. The bedroom floor even boasted a carpet – even if it was made up of mismatched pieces, patterns and colours.

Morton's face lit up. 'Look!' He exclaimed, hastening towards a wooden chest situated to the left of the window.

It was a very old chest; the wood had split and turned black, the hinges were black and pitted, and it appeared similar to those washed ashore on desert islands or discovered in dark, mysterious coves in stories of shipwrecks. Where the pirates, after hacking off the lock and lifting up the lid, discovered treasures in abundance; jewel stones sparkling on beds of gold and silver beneath disbelieving greedy eyes.

Disappointingly for Morton, there was no lock to smash from the chest, and nor was it filled with treasure but, after lifting up the lid, his eyes widened on discovering riches of a different kind.

'Come quick! Look what I've found!'

Ruth joined Morton at the chest, as Abigail entered the room.

'Look!' He implored, turning to Abigail. 'There's enough food to last weeks.'

'I'm not staying here for weeks,' Abigail said, eyeing the chest, as she stepped towards the bed.

'We might have to,' replied Morton.

'And I'm not sleeping in that,' protested Abigail, letting go of the bed sheets after a cursory inspection. Ruth and Morton were busy examining the contents of the chest and ignored her. Inside they discovered tinned foods of every kind; stewing steak, ham, corned beef, soup and broth, tins of pilchards, sardines, tuna and salmon. There were garden peas, potatoes and carrots, tins of baked beans and spaghetti in tomato sauce. There were mandarin segments in light juices, quartered peaches in heavy syrup, pineapple rings and halved pears, tins of mixed fruit with a picture of the contents on the label – a cherry prominent at the centre; and there was tins of condensed milk to accompany the fruit.

'Wow, I wish we could stay forever,' enthused Morton.

'You must be mad,' said Abigail. 'I want to go home, right now.'

'It'll be fun, you'll see,' Morton said.

'Fun, huh, and what if Bentley returns?'

Outside the blizzard raged still, and it seemed that the snow would never stop falling. The wind refused to be silenced, passing angrily over the cottage, howling and whistling to test the nerves of the sturdiest. But there, in the fragile cottage in the forest, the three young adventurers seemed condemned to spend the night. It would be the first away from their homes, removed from the protection of their parents.

CHAPTER 16

Attacked by the snow and assaulted by the wind, the old man struggled on through the blizzard and the deepening snow. Each step was more painful than the last, but he must somehow continue to summon the strength to keep going; the will to keep placing one leaden foot in front of the other. His back bent, headlong into wind and falling snow he staggered, wavering and stumbling and gasping. He craved rest and warmth but could have neither. Thoughts of his beloved cat Elsa spurred him on. She would be awaiting his return, greet him with her cheery meow and soothe his aches with her smooth tongue, her gentle purr. Should he succumb to the blizzard, the cat, shut inside the cottage, would starve and die. But he would not falter; he must not.

'Must not falter, must not,' Bentley uttered through painful lips. 'Home, Lord home, please guide me to my home.' Under the darkness and the falling snow he could barely see an outstretched hand in front of him, and with each step he sunk deeper into the snow. The snow snared his ankles, from where he must drag his foot free before he could move forwards. 'Keep going, keep going. Home, Lord home, please guide me safely to my home!'

But which way was home! Fatigued and breathless, the old man halted; he studied the ghostly shapes of the trees surrounding him, searching for clues that might indicate if he was on the right path for home. But everything everywhere looked alike; the detail all obscured by the snow. He turned, stepped tentatively forward. Stopped. Again he looked around, before setting out in a different direction. But soon he halted, frowning and shaking his head, smiling and resuming his original path, trusting in his instincts to guide him, berating himself for lingering too long in the village.

But it had been a beautiful morning; the sun warm, the wind light, the sky clear and not a single cloud in sight. The children in the village were playful and joyous; their minds focused firmly on that magical day in December when the world stood still. He had rested on the bench on the village green, listening to the children singing fragments of carols, the same carols he had sung as a child at Christmas. Bentley had sang with them…

Back bent, onwards he trudged, stumbling and fumbling through the cold dark forest. Snow clung to his clothing and turned instantly to ice; his beard was frozen and the balaclava he wore was cold and uncomfortable and chaffed his neck. His wellington boots were full of snow and his feet felt like ice, but onwards he struggled, uncertain if he walked in a straight line or in circles. Whichever direction he turned, he was confronted by the same impenetrable wall of whiteness. His heart pounded hard and erratic, and every heartbeat felt like a hammer blow that reverberated sickeningly throughout his entire body. His head throbbed and it felt as though his skull might split apart. He felt pain and dizziness, and then his vision blurred. But onwards he fought, staggering on through the snow on trembling legs, legs numb from the cold, buckling at intervals and refusing to function as they ought. And when he felt that he could go no further he stopped and rested, gasping and tottering.

Warmth and nourishment: he must have both soon or he would expire alone in the snow on the bitter night. The forest was vast and he knew not how many miles he had trod. Whether Blackdaw Cottage was near or far! Snow and darkness and the wind; it blew harder, depriving him of his breath. The snow stung his eyes and made them weep, but onwards he pressed, stumbling and staggering.

'Home. I must have my home… Must not falter, must not.' Familiar trees that might have been his guide were all alike. Shadowy objects shrouded in white, greeting him through the murk, mocking. 'Damn it, fool! Damn it!' He chanted, but self-reproach made his heart thump harder. 'Whisky, aye…' He uttered, smiling and licking his chapped lips. Concentration was lost; a leg buckled and only the deep snow prevented him from toppling over.

Energy and time ebbed away and he knew he must reach the warmth of his home soon or he would perish. Breathless and gasping, Bentley again rested, blinking the snow from bloodshot weepy eyes. And as his vision cleared, he focused on a pine tree lying at a precarious angle, resting its whitened trunk against the bough of another. He tried to imagine it from a different direction, certain the tree was the same that he looked upon each morning when he opened the door of his home. He prayed that he was right, for he knew he could not force his pain-wracked body much further. Onwards he again pushed, his step quickening when the blurred outline of a cottage came into view; Blackdaw Cottage, his home. But home was surrounded by a moat of deep snow. Had he a shovel, gaining access to his home would be easy, but he had no shovel. He clambered onto the snowdrift but sank up to his waist. Bit by bit he inched his tiring body forward. Then the smell of burning wood reached his nostrils; he smiled and looked up to the chimney and through the falling snow he witnessed smoke rising from it, corkscrewing a tortured route upwards.

'But, but…!' He remembered smothering the flames with ash before leaving his home. His breathing quickened and his heart thumped harder. Just one more push; one more stupendous effort was all that was needed to get to the other side of the snowdrift and gain access to the door of his home. But pain struck. He tottered and stumbled and a sickening dizziness caused him to retch. He knew that if he collapsed on the snow, the snow would be his tomb. Gritting his teeth, he fought harder; he pushed harder but pain, excruciating pain surged through his body and it felt as though his heart would explode. Before him stood three cottages, shifting and distorting, spawning further cottages, four, six, seven; he knew not how many. Gasping and panting, snared up to his waist in the snowdrift, he rested and waited for the pain to subside. Blinking his eyes and attempting to focus on the cottage. But which cottage, which door?

His body alternated hot and cold and the wind stole his breath. He turned from it and inhaled deeply several times, filling his lungs with reviving air, and when he next looked back, only one cottage remained. He felt relief, but was then startled by a cry. Turning, he saw Elsa, bedraggled and distressed, struggling over the snow towards him.

'Elsa!' Bentley uttered involuntarily, reaching out and touching his cat. 'But, but how…?' He looked to the cottage door and saw that it remained shut, and the windows appeared intact. Orange sparks illuminated the smoke; someone was inside the cottage stoking the fire!

'Who…?'

One last profound effort and the snowdrift collapsed. Bentley lurched forward with unexpected speed, headlong into the cottage door. The door burst open.

CHAPTER 17

It had turned six o'clock by the time Jack and his father, fatigued and cold and covered from head to foot in snow, returned to the safety of the farm with their two equally exhausted sheepdogs. But the sheep were safe, feeding on hay put out for them in the lower pastures, and should the blizzard continue into the night, any animals buried beneath the snow would be easier to locate and could be dug out quickly.

The task had taken father and son longer than anticipated, but visibility had been almost zero and it had been impossible to determine if they headed in the direction of the farm, or if they strayed into danger. Fortunately though, through Mr Evison and Jack's knowledge of the land, trees whose growth on the high pastures had been stunted, gullies, or familiar gaps in the limestone walls were all signposts that helped guide them home.

Jack whistled and the spirited dogs raced to him. The animals' shaggy coats were weighted down with icy beads that swung pendulously between their legs, impeding movement. Jack led the dogs into the stable, took out his penknife and cut the ice-balls from their coats, before feeding the hungry animals. As the dogs wolfed down their food, he prepared a warm bed of hay on which they could lay for the night. The working dogs normally slept outside in their kennels, but tonight they had earned a night of luxury inside the warm barn.

Mr Evison removed his gloves, overcoat and cap in the porch and hung them up. He opened the hall door and stepped inside shedding a further coat, which he threw on a coat stand, before heading for the kitchen.

Mrs Evison, hearing him enter, slid the kettle over the hob, and the instant the kitchen door opened she turned.

'Where –?'

'Kettle on?' Mr Evison interrupted her, rubbing his hands together.

'It's been on and off the heat for the past hour. Where's Jack and –?'

'Jack's seeing to the dogs.'

'You should have brought the poor things into the kitchen where it's warm.' She said, looking to her husband with a mixture of irritation and pride. Mr Evison walked to the cooker and sat in the chair by the side and hugged its warm enamelled sides.

Jack entered, and Mrs Evison turned to him.

'And where's Ruth?'

'Ruth?' Repeated Jack, shrugging, looking to his father. 'She's not been with us. I thought she went sledging with –?'

'Yes, yes. But I thought she might have returned earlier… Gone on the moors with you. You know what she's like.'

'She should have been back home hours ago, seeing to her chores, feeding the animals.' Mr Evison was annoyed.

'Never mind about the them,' Mrs Evison countered, her voice pitching higher and surpassing his exasperated tone. 'Ruth's out in the blizzard somewhere. Goodness knows where!'

'Well, we've not seen her,' Jack said.

The kettle boiled and Mrs Evison brewed the tea; she handed her husband and son a mug apiece. 'Surely she and her friends can't be sledging still!'

'No, no, not in this weather, and it's too dark for that. Perhaps they've got caught out and are sheltering in a barn somewhere?' Suggested Jack. 'Unless she's gone to one of her friend's homes?'

'They'll not be at Abigail's,' Mrs Evison said, with conviction. 'Mrs Markson would have phoned. And they won't be at Morton's; Ruth won't go there. So where –?'

'I'll go out… See if I can find them,' said Jack, adding more milk to his tea, standing and gulping it down.

'But where will you look, Jack?' Asked his mother. 'Ruth and her friends could be anywhere.'

'There's barns and places –'

'Have some broth first, it's ready.'

'Aye…' intervened Mr Evison. 'Let's get a hot meal inside our bellies. Ruth might show up yet. If she doesn't we'll go look for her together. It's not safe, alone in the blizzard.'

'Aye, and two could be lost as easily as one,' warned Mrs Evison.

The wind gusted hard, reminding them of the dangers, if any reminder was needed. Corrugated metal cladding and slats of wood that had worked loose on the buildings in the wind, rattled and clattered. Ruth, they knew, was always dependable; it was unlike her not to show up at a given hour. Something was wrong. Mrs Evison prayed silently that her daughter, Morton and Abigail would return home soon, for she knew that no one could survive long exposed to the bitter night. As the evening progressed, the snowstorm worsened, and somewhere three children remained lost in its fury.

CHAPTER 18

The three children sprang out from their chairs together, wide-eyed and flashing worried glances to each other, looking to the snow-covered figure prostrate on the floor. Sputnik was upon the man in a fraction of a second, barking furiously. As the dog was distracted, Elsa crept inside and hid under the table.

'Quiet, Sputnik!' Ruth bid her excitable dog.

An arm moved and outstretched fingers gestured feebly, bloodshot eyes looked pleadingly to them; eyes that Abigail had earlier looked into on the photographs on the wall.

'Help me!' Pleaded the shivering old man hoarsely.

Sputnik had ceased barking and sniffed the distressed resident of Blackdaw Cottage, wagging his tail. Bentley, after a struggle, had managed to sit up on the floor; he threaded his arms through the straps on the rucksack and released it from his back. He held out a hand.

'You get his other arm, Morton,' said Ruth, stepping towards the old man; and between them they helped Bentley to his feet. Abigail, after closing the door, carried a chair to the tottery old man and set it on the floor behind him. After lowering Bentley onto it, he began clawing his balaclava with fingers that refused to function properly. Ruth went to his aid and pulled the wet garment from his head and the mittens from his hands.

'T-t-towel!' Stuttered Bentley, shifting in his chair and pointing to a cupboard.

'I'll find one,' said Abigail, hurrying away. She opened and closed several drawers before finding one containing the towels. Returning with a towel, Bentley took it from her and used it to dry his beard and neck before handing it back to Abigail.

'Coat… Get it off me, please,' said Bentley, looking alternately to Ruth and Morton, holding out his hands. They helped him to his feet and held him steady while Abigail untied the cord from around his waist, unfastened the buttons and removed the wet coat from him.

Re-seated, Bentley pointed to his wellington boots. 'Get them off my feet, if you please.'

Abigail recoiled at the thought, but Morton held no such apprehension, crouching immediately at the old man's feet, gripping a boot and tugging. The rubber though was slippery; the boot stuck fast and it slipped through Morton's fingers. Undeterred, he re-established his grip, tugged and twisted and almost dragged Bentley from his chair, but the boot shifted suddenly, sending Morton reeling on the floor on his backside. Ruth and Abigail both laughed; Morton laughed and Bentley chuckled.

'Good lad, good lad,' he said, thrusting forward a second foot. The procedure was repeated, leaving both socks hanging from Bentley's feet; he pulled them off himself, depositing them on the growing pile of garments on the floor. 'Towel, if you please,' he next requested. Abigail handed it to him and, after drying his feet, the towel was added to the pile. 'Slippers!' Bentley then entreated, facing Ruth and pointing to the hearth. 'Fetch my slippers, if you please, good girl.' He turned to Morton. 'The whisky bottle, boy, fetch me whisky, if you please.'

Morton hurried to the cabinet, picked up the bottle with the word 'whisky' printed clearly on the label and held it aloft:

'This one?'

'Aye,' chuckled Bentley. 'If it says whisky, aye. Fetch it here, boy.' Ruth returned with the slippers and the old man put them on; he next looked to Ruth and Abigail in turn, holding out both arms: 'Girls!' Both took an arm apiece and helped the old man to his feet and, at his request, they escorted him to the fireside where they lowered him into a chair. Bentley took the whisky bottle from Morton and removed the stopper; he lifted it to his lips and swigged. 'Ah, that's better, much, much better.'

The whisky, it seemed, bestowed some kind of magical effect; after drinking some more, the old man appeared miraculously recovered. Once revitalised, his emerald eyes lit up, but he sat quietly for a while, contemplative and sipping more whisky. Then the cork stopper was replaced; hammered firmly into the bottle with blows from a flat open palm.

'Enough of that, for now,' said Bentley, handing the bottle to Abigail. 'Take it away, bonny girl, if you please.'

Abigail grabbed hold of the bottle, but Bentley did not release it immediately; he held on to the bottle for some seconds, smiling and examining her face. After noticing her unease, he chuckled and released the bottle, and Abigail took it away. He levered himself up from the chair, arresting a wobble and straightening.

'Right,' he began. 'Better have some light in here,' he said, reaching up and unhooking a lamp. He set it on the floor by the fire, got down on his knees and removed the glass dome. Sputnik, lying close by, opened an eye. 'A fine animal,' uttered Bentley, glancing to the dog, chuckling. He gripped the sooty wick between a forefinger and thumb, eased it out a little and, from a newspaper lying within reach on the floor, he tore off a strip and twisted the paper into a tight taper. The taper was pushed into the flames, and the burning taper put to the wick. A tentative blue flame flickered; it turned orange, yellowed and brightened; the expanding light lit up the room. Bentley dashed out the taper, and threw it onto the fire. The glass dome was replaced over the lamp, and the old man rose, gripping the wire handle, raising the lamp shoulder high in order to direct its flickering glow upon the children.

'Children, children,' he began with a chuckle. 'Stay put by the fire while I find some dry clothes.' He said, shuffling away towards the door that led into the adjoining room. Elsa broke cover and raced after her master, squeezing through the closing door a split second before it shut.

In Bentley's absence the children sat in silence, staring into the flames, listening to the wind as it passed over the cottage. In moments of uncertainty minutes seem like hours, and it seemed that Bentley had been absent for some time when Morton spoke.

'Maybe he's planning to murder us?'

'Don't be stupid,' Abigail said. 'Bentley wouldn't do that.'

'He might, if he was the devil.'

'Well, he looks nothing at all like the devil to me,' Abigail stressed. 'He looks –'

'That's because he's not,' cut in Ruth. 'Dad wouldn't let Bentley in his fields to catch rabbits if he was the devil.'

The door creaked open and Bentley's cat crept tentatively towards the fireside, uncertain how close to the canine visitor she dare tread. Sputnik, aware of the cat's creeping presence, raised his head and looked to her. Elsa arched her back, hissed and spat, but stood firm.

'Sputnik won't hurt you, Elsa,' laughed Ruth, leaning forward and stroking her dog, demonstrating his friendly nature. 'You won't, will you Sputnik?'

Bentley emerged from the bedroom carrying a bundle of clothes under one arm and the lighted lamp in his other. He had changed completely and was attired smartly in brown corduroy trousers; a blue checked shirt and a dark green jumper, both just visible at his neck beneath a brown leather jerkin. After lifting the lid from the corrugated metal washtub by the door, he dropped the bundle inside and replaced the wooden lid.

'I'll deal with that lot later,' said Bentley, and then shuffled across the room to the sink, where he set the lamp down on a stone slab. He turned on the tap, rinsed his hands under the running water and dried them on a towel he took from a shelf. A blackened kettle was filled with water from the same source and carried to the fire, where it was hooked on the metal arm and lowered over the flames. Bentley held up the lamp.

'A bonny bunch, aye' he chuckled, 'Ruth Evison, I know you, know all your family. Your father's a gentleman and your mother's a kind lady, and your brother.' He halted and pondered. 'His name escapes me…'

'Jack,' Ruth reminded him.

'Aye, that's it, Jack,' smiled Bentley. 'A handsome, hardworking young man.' He turned to Morton. 'And I know you, young Morton Rymer… A spirited boy, aye.' His eyes next alighted upon Abigail, and they shifted rapidly in their sockets, as he looked her up and down. She turned from his gaze, glancing fitfully back to determine if his stare remained. 'Young lady.' He at last spoke, contemplative and stroking his beard. 'I know nothing at all of you, yet feel that I ought.' He shuffled closer. 'What name, bonny girl?'

Abigail raised her head: 'Abigail.' She replied.

'Abigail! Abigail who? Your surname?'

'Markson. It's Abigail Markson,' she answered firmly and in a manner that suggested he should be familiar with her family. They had, after all, been resident in the small community for eight months.

'Markson.' Bentley repeated the name, as he tugged

his beard. 'No, never heard of a Markson before.' He said, turning from her; but then he turned swiftly back and a smile stretched his lips. 'But wait, I have seen you before… Walking out to the shops with your mother, aye, now I remember. Your mother, aye… Know her.' The old man reached up and hung the lamp on the wire hook. The shifting light from the swinging lamp projected a distorted, lumbering image of him on the walls and ceiling, as he shuffled towards the fire. He threw on several more logs before sitting. Sighing, he faced the three children.

'Well, what trouble now!' He suddenly said in a severe tone, and when he leaned forward abruptly, Morton flinched. 'Absent from your families. Breaking into my home.' He pointed to the peanut shells scattered about the hearth. 'Eating my food!'

'But we… We never meant any harm,' began Abigail. 'It was snowing really heavily and we had to shelter somewhere, or we might die. But we'll go –'

'Go!' Interrupted Bentley, sternly. 'Go where? Where will you go?'

Abigail shrugged and looked to him with a forlorn gaze. 'Don't know.'

'Think I'm a heartless old devil, do you, eh?' His tone was firm and the chuckle that followed indeed sounded sinister. 'Wicked enough to turn young children from my home into a raging blizzard?' He paused, shook his head and his tone softened, he chuckled warmly. 'No, bonny girl, you and your friends are going nowhere tonight.'

'But you won't murder us, will you?' Questioned Morton.

'Murder you!' Bentley sounded exasperated. 'I kill nothing that I don't eat.'

Morton gulped: 'But you're not a cannibal, are you? You're not going to kill us and eat us, are you?'

'Kill you! Eat you!' Bentley licked his lips; he leaned closer to the children, grinning impishly. 'Think little boys and girls might make a tasty meal, do you?' Fear widened their eyes, but Bentley could maintain his deceit no longer and broke into laughter, loud uproarious laughter. 'What! Murder you! Eat you! Who the devil have you been listening to, eh? Vargis, that fool of a gamekeeper?'

The children were at first unsure whether to laugh, cry, or flee the cottage and take their chance in the blizzard. But Bentley calmed his laughter:

'I've harmed no human being that I'm aware of… Never.' He looked at Sputnik lying peacefully on the hearth. 'And I wouldn't turn a dog out on a night like tonight.'

'But we didn't break into your house,' Ruth said. 'The door wasn't locked. And dad'll pay if –'

'Dad won't pay,' cut in Bentley. 'I've no interest in money – never did have. I've enough to live on and I don't need more. But you children must take more care in future, straying from the village during a blizzard!'

'It wasn't snowing when we went sledging,' Ruth informed him.

'No, I dare say it wasn't,' Bentley agreed. 'And the blizzard caught me out – nearly saw the death of me, and might have if… But, but think of your poor parents. They'll not know if you're safe or buried beneath the snow.'

'Dad'll be mad, I know he will,' Morton said, sniffing. 'I didn't wash up and I didn't sweep the floor –'

'And mum'll be worried,' interrupted Abigail. 'I've never stayed anywhere before without mum or dad.' She said, cheerlessly. 'And I promised…'

Abigail was right to think that her mother would be worried; any caring parent would be concerned for children who failed to return home while a blizzard raged.

Had Mrs Markson any inclination that her daughter was about to spend the night in the ramshackle cottage in the cold forest with a man she detested, she would have been mortified; compelled, perhaps, to arm herself with a shovel and dig a path through the snow to the door of Blackdaw Cottage.

'Well, well, children,' began Bentley. 'Fate has thrown us together and we must make the best of it; accept what we cannot alter, try and gain some enjoyment from each other's company.'

As he spoke, the tempo of the wind increased; the door banged and the window frames rattled and it seemed the combined forces might turn the frail cottage into a pile of rubble. Snow was forced inside through unseen fissures, the ultra-fine crystals hung in the air like a mist, before succumbing to gravity and accumulating in a growing white mound on the floor. But Bentley was not afraid; he had witnessed nature's hostile power before, and Blackdaw Cottage, he remained confident, would again repel the worst that nature had to offer, demonstrate its resilience and defend all who remained within its four walls, keep them safe throughout the night. The children's stomachs rumbled, Bentley's stomach rumbled and he chuckled.

'Well, who's hungry?' He asked.

The children nodded together, but it was Ruth that spoke first.

'I'm starving,' she said. 'And I'm thirsty.'

'Have you got any chicken?' Morton enquired boldly.

'Chicken!' Repeated Bentley, chuckling. Ruth and Abigail smiled expectantly; roast chicken was their favourite too. 'I'm afraid chicken is off today's menu, children, but never mind…' He shuffled to the edge of his seat rubbing his hands together and lowering his voice. 'If you can keep a little secret –'

'But it's wrong to…' Abigail began sternly, but fell silent instantly when Ruth and Morton turned their indignation upon her.

'…I've a pheasant marinating in a pot, ready to pop into the oven.'

'You've stolen one of Vargis's pheasants!' Morton was exasperated.

'Shhh, children, survival! We must eat what's available. And that fool Vargis has poisoned the rabbits – spread a plague among them – and we can't eat poisoned meat, can we?' Steam began to stream from the kettle's spout and Bentley stood. 'Who'd like a hot drink?'

The children each nodded.

'Cocoa! Do you all like cocoa?'

The children again nodded.

Bentley proceeded to remove a cloth from the pocket of his jerkin; he arranged it in a palm and, using it to protect his hands from the heat, he lifted the kettle from the hook and set off across the floor with it, chuckling. After setting the kettle down on the stone slab, he procured a blackened cooking pot, removed the lid and poured in boiling water, before stirring the contents with a spoon. The lid was replaced, the pot carried to the oven and pushed inside.

'There we are, children, pheasant casserole,' smiled Bentley, chuckling as he shuffled away. He lined up four mugs and then, using the handle of a teaspoon, prised the lid off a tin. From it he spooned a measure of cocoa powder into each mug, and turned.

'Sugar, children?'

'Yes, please,' Ruth and Abigail answered together.

'Lots for me,' Morton called out.

'Lots!' Repeated Bentley, chuckling. 'Lots for all…'

Boiling water was poured into the mugs, milk was

added, and the remaining water was emptied into an enamelled bowl in the sink. The mugs were placed onto a wooden tray and carried to the awaiting children.

'Cocoa, madams, is served,' he said frivolously, lowering the tray in front of the girls. Ruth and Abigail picked up a mug apiece. 'Be very careful, it's scalding hot.' He warned, turning to Morton. 'Sir...' He picked it up, and Bentley took the remaining mug and joined the children around the blazing fire. Ruth, Abigail and Morton were safe; they were warm and as comfortable as could be expected given the circumstances. But consciences remained troubled, and the three children, separated from their families during the worst snowstorm the country had witnessed in years, were concerned not only for themselves but for their parents, sitting in their homes, knowing not if their precious offspring were alive or had become victims of the blizzard. The stranded adventurers, though, could do nothing other than endure what they must; suffer what uncomfortable thoughts might invade their waking hours, infiltrate their dreams and await morning. But the night had first to be survived.

CHAPTER 19

Mr Evison and Jack held on to hope and were confident that the children could be found that night. They stepped from the farmhouse together and the bitter wind greeted them with a powerful gust that might have sent lesser men into retreat, but both were determined; the lives of young children were in danger. After tightening their clothing they picked up a shovel each and strode on in defiance of the blizzard. It was not until they stepped from the shelter provided by the farm buildings that the full force of the storm was felt, chilling them to the bone in seconds. Onwards the men battled, two insignificant white figures swimming in a white ocean.

The men reached the road that passed through the village. It was completely deserted; whom, though, but the foolhardy or desperate souls on a desperate mission would step out into such a tempestuous night? The pair waded on through knee-deep snow, crossed the road and climbed over a style, jumping down into thigh-high snow on the other side. They battled on across exposed pastures, fighting against the wind – a wind that gusted so hard at times it brought the men to a standstill. If only the snow was less deep! If they could see where they were going! If wind did not blow! If the snow did not fall! Heads down, onwards the men pressed, staggering like drunks, guided by the vague contours of the land, the line of wall or a broken fence, the position of a gate, a tree until the signposts became obscured and instinct was all they had to rely upon.

At last the shadowy image of a barn presented itself through the obfuscating screen of white, lifting their spirits – the children might be inside sheltering. Jack reached the building ahead of his father and attempted to look inside through the gap where the huge twin oak doors met. He could see or hear nothing, and began shovelling the snow away from the doors. The snow swirled viciously about him, and as fast as he cleared it away the wind blew it back; it was only when father and son worked together that their combined efforts proved a match for the elements. A door was prised open and the frozen men squeezed inside. But expectation succumbed to disappointment; the barn was empty and there was no evidence of children having ever entered. Exhausted, the men rested a while, blowing hot breaths into cupped hands and stamping their feet on the earthen floor in order to restore circulation to frozen toes.

'Come on, dad,' urged Jack, picking up his shovel, hesitating and looking outside, before forcing his body back out between the twin doors. Mr Evison followed. The barn doors were secured and the men set out in search of the next building. It was a dangerous mission and frozen bodies struggle to function as they should; minds become disorientated and hypothermia remains an ever-present threat. The men were aware of the dangers, but knew that the children must be found and got home quickly.

Other barns were located and searched – some twice in the confusion – each yielding the same disappointing result. Disillusionment began to depress the men's spirits, and the blizzard worsened. The wind grew increasingly hostile, whipping the snow up from the ground and swirling it into a mesmerising cauldron that neither men could see through.

'This is hopeless, Jack. It's madness, it'll be the death of us!' Mr Evison, in some distress, said. 'We're not going to find Ruth and her friends tonight. We should get home quick or we'll perish ourselves.'

'Jackson's barn!' Jack called back, hopefully. 'We've not looked there yet.'

'But we've not found it!'

'We've got to try.'

'All right, Jack, but no more. I'm all but done for.'

Jack stumbled upon a gate he knew led into the yard where Jackson's barn was located – that was their only bit of good fortune. Mr Evison, by now though, was hardly able to lift a shovel; he watched as his son shovelled the snow away from the barn doors, becoming interested only when Jack halted suddenly and pressed an ear to the door.

'Ruth!' Jack called out, jabbing the blade of the shovel between the twin doors, attempting to prise them open, calling her name again and listening. His animation proved infectious; his father summoning sufficient strength to assist, gripping the door and tugging, while Jack chipped away the ice. The door finally shifted; its hinges creaked and a gap widened.

'Ruth! Ruth, are you in there?' Mr Evison, animated, called. His elation was brief. 'Sheep! Jackson's bloody sheep.' He uttered dejectedly.

The neighbouring farmer, it seemed, had been better informed of the approaching adverse weather and had gathered his sheep from the fields and fastened them inside the barn, where they would be safe. Mr Evison and Jack stepped into the barn anyway. The warm musty air was welcome nourishment to shivering bodies. The bleating sheep surrounded the men, looking expectantly to them, but Mr Evison and Jack had nothing to offer the inquisitive animals.

'Where's it all coming from?' Mr Evison questioned, looking outside at the falling snow. Many people had shared the same thoughts and had asked the same question. Snow fell relentlessly; it had done so since late afternoon. Snow lay knee-deep throughout the land, but in places where it had drifted, snow was deep enough to bury a man standing six feet tall. It fell still, and the drifting snow began to swallow up entire houses.

Mr Evison and Jack's mission had yielded only disappointment and growing despair, and it was with an overwhelming sense of defeat the exhausted men headed home. All buildings where the children might have been sheltering had been searched, and now their own lives were becoming increasingly imperilled. They turned for home into a strengthening wind; a wind that at times hurried the men forward faster than their tired legs could work, forcing them face down upon the cold snow.

The weary men were relieved when they reached the main road, even though they had strayed some distance from their intended route. If, on reaching the road, the men expected to find respite from the blizzard, they were wrong. Snow was driven at them at speed from over walls and hawthorn bushes, gathering in deep drifts and slowing them down. They had not progressed far along the road when Mr Evison, gasping for breath and faltering, halted.

'You go on ahead, Jack,' he urged.

'No, dad, no.' Jack responded firmly, taking his father's arm, slinging it over his shoulder and hauling him along. 'I'm not leaving you here.'

'I'm done for, son. You go, Jack. Go and fetch the tractor, I can't walk any further.'

'It's too deep for the tractor, and if I abandoned you here you'd be buried beneath the snow before I returned.'

Jack knew that if he left his father the snow would become his tomb; the snow would be the tomb of them both if they did not hurry home. They were frozen, weakening with every step, but onward they struggled. Jack dragging his father with him as best he could, knowing that one false step would propel them into death's awaiting embrace.

CHAPTER 20

Seated around the blazing fire at Blackdaw Cottage, the three children and Bentley faced no such perils. For them, the night held no trying trials at all other than the trivialities of coexistence in the modest cottage in the forest. Sputnik rested blissfully at the feet of Ruth. Elsa, sat close by, having accepted the presence of the uninvited canine, preened her white coat. She remained watchful and alert, though, and each time Sputnik twitched Elsa flinched.

'Don't you get frightened living alone in the forest?' Abigail asked Bentley.

'No, never,' he replied. 'There's nothing to be afraid of in the forest. Few people pass this way. My only regular visitor is Vargis, the gamekeeper.' He chuckled. 'The old fool turns up uninvited, posturing with his gun… Thinks I ought to be afraid of him, thinks he's someone important with a shotgun in his hand. He annoys me, that's all.' The old man lifted the mug to his lips and sipped. Licking his lips, he turned to the trio. 'Well, children, I fear it'll be a long and dreary night for you. What are we to do to while away the hours?'

The children, looking to their host, remained tight-lipped, hopeful that he might introduce them to an ancient form of entertainment – a game that he perhaps played as a child. Bentley continued:

'I've nothing here to amuse children, no games, no radio or television – none of those newfangled contraptions.'

'Books!' Abigail said abruptly. 'You must have books?'

'Books!' Bentley and Morton exclaimed together.

Bentley smiled, but Morton frowned.

'Yes, I like to listen to stories,' continued Abigail. 'Mum used to read to me at bedtime when I was little. But now she says I must read for myself.'

'And quite right, too,' agreed Bentley. 'You're old enough – clever enough, I'm sure.'

'Yes, but it's much better when somebody else reads the story.'

'Better… Easier, I dare say,' laughed Bentley. 'Well, I confess the only book in my possession is the Bible.'

'The Bible!' Exclaimed Morton, somewhat mortified.

'Aye, and I've not turned its pages in years. I've little inclination these days – little able to since my eyesight began to fail. And I've little time.'

'But you can get free spectacles on the National Health,' Ruth advised him.

Bentley laughed. 'Indeed, and I own a pair, but… Well, vanity.'

'The Bible!' Morton's disillusionment grumbled on. He was appalled at the thought of being made to sit and listen to extracts read from the religious text. 'My teacher makes everyone in class read aloud from the bible, and it's boring. Dad says it's a load of rubbish, he says –'

'Young man,' interrupted Bentley. 'You should study the good book and learn from it. Use it as a template for a virtuous life.'

'A virtuous life!' Morton repeated, frowning. 'I'd rather build a snowman.'

'Well, I'm not building any stupid snowmen,' Abigail insisted.

'No, no,' agreed Bentley. 'I think we'd better find entertainment indoors tonight, we've seen enough snow for one day – more than enough.'

'Well, I shall build a snowman tomorrow,' Morton was

determined. 'Lots of snowmen if we have to stay here for weeks.'

'Weeks!' Bentley exclaimed.

'But we'll be able to go home tomorrow, won't we?' Asked Abigail.

'I don't want to go home tomorrow,' Morton said, somewhat glumly. 'I don't ever want to go home.'

'Don't want to go home?' Repeated Bentley, somewhat mystified.

'But why not?' Asked Abigail. Then she remembered the earlier revelations about his uncomfortable relationship with his father; she nipped her lips together and fell silent.

'Dad'll be mad, I know he will. I didn't polish his shoes, I didn't wash up and I didn't sweep the kitchen floor, and I, I…' And there Morton faltered and halted.

'But your father will be relieved, surely…? Happy to see his son safely back home,' Bentley said, in an attempt to reassure Morton. 'He'll not care about shoes left unpolished and dirty floors.'

But Morton was not reassured: 'I'm never going home, not ever.' He stressed.

Ruth looked to Morton. Her friend's sadness was palpable. She more than anyone knew why her friend would rather remain absent from home. It was for the same reason he had many times expressed a desire to live on the farm with Ruth. But, unlike Morton, Ruth would much prefer the company of her own family in the security of her own home, and she knew that her parents and Jack would be worried by her absence. Ruth looked to Sputnik, and her heart gladdened; she was happy he was with her. In fact, all eyes were now focused on the animals lying peacefully together. Both the cat and dog remained alert, though, reacting to every sound inside or out, with a twitch of an ear of a rotation of an eyeball. Bentley, observing his cat's reaction when Sputnik yawned, chuckled:

'What's the matter, Elsa?' The animal cat cast her tired gaze in his direction, starting when the dog moved to scratch his belly. 'Sputnik won't bite you.' He laughed.

Both animals sprang to their feet when the wind gusted with determined force, rattling the door and window frames. Bentley, noticing the hessian curtain dancing in the wind and seeing snow forced inside, set his mug down on the floor. He rose and, after straightening with a grimace, set off in jerky steps towards the window. Inactivity after the earlier trials in the blizzard had stiffened his rheumatic joints, and every step was a triumph of the will over a reluctant body.

He drew the curtain aside and used it to wipe the window, but he could see nothing outside through the snow-covered glass panes. Snow blew about his legs; he turned, bent down and picked the bundle of rags up from the floor and stuffed them back into the hole from where they had been displaced. The hessian sacking was allowed to fall back into place and it stirred no more. The wind and snow had been sealed out for the night – or so it was hoped.

CHAPTER 21

The snow was unrelenting; the wind blew stronger and colder, buffeting the two men like a boxer pummelling a dispirited opponent with strength-sapping blows, but onwards the men staggered. Jack re-tightened his grip over his faltering father, half-dragging and half-carrying him along, but he too was now beginning to weaken.

'Go Jack. Save yourself. I can't walk any fur…' The wind stole his breath and he turned from it, gasping and coughing. 'I can't walk any further. For God's sake, go.'

'I'm not leaving you here. Come on, dad.' Jack urged, hauling his father on through the deepening snow.

Both men were frozen; they were soaked to the skin and shivered continually. It was agony; each second felt like a minute, each minute an hour and as the cold bit deeper into the sinews of their bodies their minds became confused. Images appeared through the murkiness and noises; muffled voices struggling to make their presence heard above the roar of the wind. Before them a lumbering figure loomed closer – the reaper scything the weak, the faltering – and a bounding white animal at his side. Fear struck and father and son halted.

'What in the name of the devil are you fools doing?'

It was the gamekeeper and his dog Jet. The black labrador was white from the snow and the gamekeeper was unrecognisable within the hood and scarf that covered much of his face, but his voice was unmistakable.

'We're not poaching pheasants, for sure,' Jack said. 'What about you?'

'Birds to feed,' was the gamekeeper's curt reply.

Why, in the grip of the blizzard, was anyone's guess.

Corn thrown down to the birds would be lost to the snow in seconds unless the pheasants were adept and able to pluck the grain out of the air.

'Good God, man!' Ejaculated Vargis, seeing Jack struggling to hold his father upright. 'Better get him home quick.' He urged, taking Mr Evison's right arm and hoisting it over his shoulder. 'Come on, Jack, let's get him home, sod your damn sheep.'

'It's not the sheep,' Jack informed him. 'It's Ruth. She and her friends, Morton and Abigail; they went sledging this afternoon and haven't returned. We've looked in all the barns –'

'Damn fools... Saw them playing in the forest this afternoon. I sent them home, or so I thought... Blighters, they must have doubled back.'

'We've been looking in the wrong place, dad,' Jack said to his father. 'Did you hear? Mr Vargis said Ruth and her friends were in the forest this afternoon.'

Mr Evison, after digesting the significance of the information Jack communicated to him, nodded. 'They'll find scant shelter in the forest.'

'There's only the cottage, Bentley's cottage,' Jack reminded him. 'If they've got that far.'

'Aye, and they'd be safer building an igloo and sheltering in that than living under the same roof as that old devil,' Vargis said.

'Bentley wouldn't harm them, would he?' Jack asked.

'No, no... Don't suppose he would.' Vargis said, noticing Jack's anguish. 'No, Bentley wouldn't harm children. And there they'd have a roof over their heads. But it'd not do for me... Sleeping under the same roof as that old rogue.'

Mr Evison managed to smile through his pain: 'Ruth would probably find it fun – an adventure.'

'I'll set out for the cottage as soon as we've got you home, dad.'

'Damn it, no, Jack!' Vargis bid him. 'It'd be madness, suicidal. Wait until morning. If the children are at the cottage, they'll be fine. If not, well…'

'He's right, Jack,' agreed Mr Evison. 'No sense getting yourself killed. No one can do anything for the children now before morning.'

'Hopefully the snow will have stopped by then,' the gamekeeper said. He turned to Mr Evison and Jack. 'Come, let's get a move on, or the three of us will be stiffs before daybreak.'

The farm remained some distance away, presenting the men with a formidable challenge under the hostile blizzard and the deepening snow. Their pace was slow and Vargis and Jack practically carried Mr Evison between them. But onwards they struggled, fighting against the might of the bitter night.

CHAPTER 22

Bentley stoked the fire and sparks leapt up through the tongues of orange flame, disappearing up the chimney. Abigail, deep in thought and watching, allowed her mind to wander, wishing desperately that she could be transported magically back to her own home; to her own family. Her wish could not be granted that night, and her suffering was the price for their folly, for the torment that she had unwittingly unleashed upon her parents. A tear spilled from her eye and onto her cheek; she raised a hand and swiftly wiped it away, hoping that no one had noticed.

'If only I could tell mum,' she blurted suddenly. 'Let her know I'm safe.'

'No chance of that,' said Bentley, laying the poker down on the hearth and turning to her. 'What's done cannot be undone tonight, bonny girl.' He smiled. 'But dinner will be ready soon, and you'll feel better with hot food in your belly, we all will.'

Indeed, the aroma from pheasant casserole cooking in the oven had already sharpened Morton's appetite. 'I'm starving,' he said.

'So am I,' said Ruth.

'Good, good,' chuckled Bentley. 'Children with appetites…' Pointing, he faced Morton. 'Fetch me the wooden spoon, if you please, young man.' He said, removing a cloth from the pocket of his jerkin

Morton was at the cabinet in a flash, pulling open a drawer and rummaging through the utensils. He found a wooden spoon and held up for approval. 'This one?'

'Aye, if it's a spoon and it's made of wood, aye,' chuckled Bentley. 'And look sharp about it.'

Ruth and Abigail watched their host fold the cloth in half and arrange it between both hands. He opened the range door, reached inside and lifted out the casserole and set it down on the hearth. He removed the lid and stirred the contents with the spoon Morton handed to him. Chunks of meat and vegetables surfaced from beneath the rich dark gravy before re-submerging.

'I hope you'll all like pheasant casserole?'

'I do,' said Ruth, stroking her dog. 'And so does Sputnik, don't you, boy? Mum makes it sometimes when Vargis gives dad a pheasant.'

Bentley replaced the lid and the pot was pushed back inside the oven. 'A few more minutes,' he said, chuckling.

'Does pheasant taste like chicken?' Asked Abigail. 'I like chicken.'

'Aye...' Replied Bentley somewhat tentatively, whilst stroking his beard. 'Aye, I dare say pheasant does taste rather like chicken.' He smiled wryly. Pheasant meat, he knew, was darker than chicken and its flavour was stronger and it tasted altogether unlike chicken, but he felt that if Abigail was sufficiently hungry she would neither recognise the difference nor care. In any case, the flavour of the pheasant would be masked after absorbing the flavours from the vegetables and herbs in which the bird had been marinated and cooked.

'Did you shoot the pheasant?' Enquired Morton.

'No, no,' Bentley replied, sitting. 'I've never owned a gun in my life... Wouldn't have one in the house. No... I was one day watching the pheasants feeding on some crusts I'd thrown out, when Elsa appeared suddenly. The pheasants took fright and one poor blighter flew into the house wall... Snapped its neck clean in two.' He chuckled, mischievously. 'No point wasting good, fresh meat, I thought. So I picked the bird up, carried it inside, plucked it, dressed it, chopped it up and popped it into a pot with herbs, onions, potatoes, turnips, leeks, carrots, salt and pepper.' He said, and then burst unexpectedly into laughter, startling the children. 'I wish that grumpy old fool, Vargis, was here to witness us tuck into his pheasant.'

'Why do you wish Vargis was here?' Asked Abigail, somewhat bemused.

'For fun!' Bentley enthused. 'For fun, bonny girl, to plague the bad-tempered hypocrite. He'd go mad, I'm sure, shoot me – shoot us all if he dare.'

'I don't want to be shot,' said Abigail sternly, shifting uneasily in her chair at the thought of Vargis arriving and murdering them as they sat feasting on pheasant casserole. 'But Vargis won't really shoot us, will he?'

'No, no,' chuckled Bentley. 'I don't suppose he would... Like to shoot me, perhaps, but no...'

It was unlikely that Vargis or anyone else would be visiting them at Blackdaw Cottage that night. No one would be able to find the cottage while the blizzard continued. Snow lay deep on the ground, it continued to deepen; and even if the snow should cease to fall at that instant it would take half a day or more to reach Blackdaw Cottage.

'Don't you like Vargis?' Morton asked Bentley.

'Like him! The man's a fool... Blames me for all that's wrong in the forest. Every fallen branch he thinks I've cut down for firewood, every dead pheasant, he thinks I've killed. But it's not my nature to hate, and I dislike him only because he despises me. I like to have fun... Torment him until he's hopping mad.'

'Vargis is always angry,' said Abigail.

'Aye, you're right, bonny girl,' agreed Bentley. 'He's forever shouting, aiming that blasted gun of his at some poor creature. I'd like to snatch it from him and –'

'He shouted at us this afternoon,' interrupted Ruth. 'Told us to go home, but we didn't go home because we don't like doing what he tells us.'

'Well, for once it would have been wise to follow his advice,' Bentley said. 'But never mind, you're safe.'

'We didn't know it was going to snow all day, did we?' Said Ruth.

'No, no, you couldn't have known,' decided Bentley. 'No one knew the snow would arrive so suddenly... Fall so heavily. It caught me out also.'

'I hope it caught Vargis out, as well,' Abigail said with passion. 'He's horrible and cruel, and he shot a bird.'

'He'll shoot anything that moves,' said Bentley. 'You should think yourselves lucky he didn't mistake you for a fox – for me! I'll one day snatch that gun from him and wrap it round his blasted neck.'

'And he's always spitting,' added Abigail. 'He's horrid.'

'Aye, the man should be locked away from decent people.'

'In a prison?' Morton asked.

'A Prison! And who'd want to share a cell with Mr Hector Vargis? No, he should be shipped away... Kicked off on an island where life doesn't exist.'

'But then he'd starve!' Abigail decided.

'He could eat grass... Chew the tree roots.' Laughed Bentley. He gripped the arms of the chair and stood. 'Vargis is an ill-tempered, selfish fool.' He grimaced and groaned as he straightened. 'This weather, it fair plagues my lumbago.' The old man then carried plates and the butter dish to the fireside and set them down on the hearth to warm, the butter to soften.

The children were at ease and no longer afraid of the strange old man. In Bentley, they saw a kindly old man of whom life had treated harshly. Ruth rose from her chair and stepped to the window; she pulled the hessian curtain aside and pushed her head to the glass, but snow covered the small square windows, blotting out the outside world completely.

'Has it stopped snowing yet, Ruth?' Asked Abigail.

'I can't see out, but I don't think it has. It'll be ten feet deep by tomorrow.'

'Ten feet deep!' Exclaimed Morton. The heightened pitch of his voice articulated his degree of excitement. 'We'll be able to stay here for weeks.'

'I don't want to stay for weeks,' Abigail said, dismally. 'I want to go home.'

'We won't be here for weeks. Dad and Jack'll come tomorrow, you'll see,' Ruth said confidently, rejoining her friends by the fireside. She stood a while, warming her back on the fire.

'Gather the mugs, Ruth, if you please, Miss Evison,' Bentley called out, noticing her standing. 'I've filled a bowl with hot, soapy water. Come girl, make yourself useful and then we'll feed the animals.'

Ruth smiled; she knew that Sputnik would be hungry and willingly gathered the pots and carried them to the sink. She pushed up her sleeves and submerged the pots under the hot water.

'Good girl, good girl,' said Bentley, handing her other items that needed washing. He pointed. 'There are clean towels for drying the pots… Towels for your hands.'

Ruth faced him and smiled: 'Do you like living in the forest?'

'I do indeed. It's a hard life and wouldn't suit everyone. But for me there's no place quite like it on earth. I'm relaxed here – at peace with the world, in the company of the birds and animals; the air is fresh. I've lived here much my adult life, and here I'll die.'

Elsa interrupted their conversation, meowing repeatedly. The cat knew that feeding time was nigh and rubbed the length of her body along Bentley's legs, her tail was erect and rigid, the tip twitching like a rattlesnake's tail. Bentley turned from his cat to Ruth.

'I'm an old man now,' he began. 'My life is almost done, and my sole wish is to be allowed to live out my life in my home – to be buried in the forest earth. Given that assurance, I'll die the happiest man can on departing from this planet.'

'But you're no going to die yet, are you? And no one's going to kick you out of your home, will they?'

'No, no, let's hope not.' Elsa's meowing grew frenetic. 'Impatient girl! Wait a minute.' Bentley said, handing a dish of the scraps to Ruth. 'Vargis, I'm sure, would see me driven from my home if he could, but I'll not submit to the likes of him. I'd provoke him to shoot me first.'

'But you must get lonely sometimes?' Ruth said.

'No, never. In all the years I've lived in my forest home, never have I once felt alone.' Bentley became thoughtful. 'In fact, the only time I felt truly alone was when I was young man in a city full of strangers. That, for me, is loneliness.' He smiled and lowered the dish to the floor. The cat tucked into her food. 'And I've Elsa for company,' he added, his smile widening as he watched his cat feeding.

'Sputnik!' Ruth called out, and her dog raced to her, startling the cat who arched her back and hissed. 'Sputnik won't harm you, Elsa. He's a hungry animal, like you.'

The dog wolfed down the scraps of food in little time and stood licking his jowls, watching the cat eat. Thankfully, there were no further outbreaks of animosity between the two animals from then on; enemies had all became friends.

CHAPTER 23

Watching the two animals enjoying their food sharpened Ruth's appetite. 'I'm hungry,' she said, rejoining Bentley at the sink.

'Good, good,' he smiled, shaking drops of water from his hands, standing aside to allow Ruth access to the bowl of water, taking a towel and drying his hands. He turned: 'and you two, are you hungry too?'

'I'm starving,' Morton said. 'Is it ready yet?'

'Soon, soon.'

'I'm a little hungry,' Abigail said, somewhat unconvincingly. In truth, she longed for home and for the familiar safe taste of her mother's cooking.

'Good girl, good girl.'

Ruth watched Bentley remove the lid from a green enamelled breadbin situated in a corner on the stone slab. He reached inside and took out a brown loaf, which he set on a wooden board and, after removing a serrated bladed knife from a drawer, began slicing the loaf.

'The butter, if you please,' Bentley said, turning to Ruth. 'And mind, the dish might be hot!' He chuckled, and continued cutting slices from the loaf.

'Shall I butter the slices?' Ruth asked, returning with the butter.

Bentley smiled: 'I see your mother's made a fine job of teaching you. Aye, spread the butter on nice and thick… Need extra fat this weather to help fight off the cold.'

Ruth removed the lid from the butter dish, took the blunt-bladed knife that Bentley handed her, and stroked the blade over the softened yellow spread, loading it with butter and applying a generous layer to the thick slices of bread. She arranged the buttered slices neatly on a rectangular blue and white patterned plate. Ruth had many times assisted her mother with the same task in their farmhouse kitchen, often receiving a mild rebuke for her too-liberal ways with the butter.

The entire loaf was sliced, the slices all buttered and dinner was another step closer. Even Abigail's appetite began to sharpen, as the tempting aroma of the pheasant casserole simmering in the oven permeated the room.

'I'm quite hungry now,' she said to Morton. 'Though I'm not sure if I should like pheasant casserole.'

'Well, I'm starving. I could eat almost anything,' he said, looking enviously to Ruth helping herself to a crust. Bentley looked to her and chuckled:

'Bread to the table, if you please, Miss Evison, before you eat it all. And while you're there, set the table… Spoons are in the drawer… Dishes warming by the fire.' He said, taking a towel and setting off in hurried short steps towards the cooking range.

Ruth stuffed the remainder of the crust of bread into her mouth and brushed the crumbs from her hands, before carrying the plate of bread to the table. She retrieved the warmed dishes from the hearth, procured spoons from a drawer and set four places at the table. Morton and Abigail's eyes were focused upon Bentley who arranged the towel between his hands, opened the range door and lifted out the casserole.

'Come… Sir, madam, dinner is about to be served,' he said frivolously, smiling at the children and shuffling towards the table with the casserole dish. 'The ladle, Miss Evison, fetch me the ladle, if you please.' He said, setting the dish down on the table, lifting off lid and inhaling the fragrant steam that rose from the casserole. 'Delicious, I'm sure,' he chuckled. Morton and Abigail sat together on one side of the table; Ruth sat down opposite Abigail. 'It's as well I've three hungry children dining with me tonight; there's more food than I could eat in a week.' After a brief stir, Bentley divided the casserole between the four dishes and a dish was pushed in front of each child.

'Tuck in, children, tuck in. Careful, though! It's scalding hot!' The old man warned. He looked upon the children with the fondness he might had they been grandchildren of his own. His face beamed; he felt confident that the dish he had prepared would prove acceptable and satisfy the fickle tastes of young children. He sat down on the chair next to Ruth. 'I'm sure it's no match for your mothers' cooking, but will it do?'

The three stuffed mouths were incapable of replying orally; with puffed-out smiling faces, each child nodded, communicating their gratitude more eloquently than words ever could. The pheasant casserole, Bentley hoped, would prove sufficient and help to sustain the lives of the three young children throughout the impending cold night. He picked up a slice of bread, dipped it in the juices, bit into it, tasted and smiled. His greatest pleasure, though, was in observing the joyous faces of the children feasting on the fruits of his labours.

The night would be the longest of the children's short lives. Fate had delivered the misguided adventurers into his hands, and Bentley felt duty-bound to ensure that none would succumb to the cruel night. But more, much more, remained to be done.

CHAPTER 24

Jack led his shivering father into the porch and Vargis, supporting the faltering man from behind, closed the door. The hall door opened and Mrs Evison appeared, shaking her head and looking to the men with a degree of severity that was at odds with her normal placid demeanour.

'Just look at you!' Her ire was directed at her husband and Jack, but then she saw the gamekeeper following behind and her tone softened; she forced a smile. 'Mr Vargis…'

'Mrs Evison,' the gamekeeper responded, nodding.

'It's worse out there than we thought, mum,' said Jack, in an effort to appease her, offer some kind of explanation for the distressed state of his father.

'Well you're back, thank God,' Mrs Evison said. 'Get your wet coats off quickly, and get your father into the kitchen where it's warm. And what about –?'

'Ruth?' Interposed Jack. 'No sign of her,' he added, despondently, shaking his head.

'Well, let's hope she's more sense than… Well, let's hope that she and her friends have found somewhere safe to shelter or else…' The 'or else' was too dreadful to contemplate; and Mrs Evison could not bring herself to complete the sentence. Jack, looking to her, frowned; had it not been for the reckless adventure embarked upon by his sister and her two friends, he and his father would not have been forced out into the blizzard that night in the first place, risking their lives.

'Is the kettle on, mum?'

'It's been on and off the hob for the past hour, and more,' she responded, irritably still as she tugged the buttons apart on her husband's overcoat, pulled the icy coat from him.

'Mr Vargis thinks Ruth and her friends might have gone to the cottage,' Jack informed her.

'Gone to the cottage! Blackdaw Cottage! Well, why? What on earth were they thinking? Traipsing all that way in the snow!' Mrs Evison noticed Vargis struggling to unfasten the buttons on his coat and went to his aid.

'Thank you, Mrs Evison, thank –'

'Get your father's boots off, Jack.' Mrs Evison barked, turning to her son. 'And get him into the kitchen, for goodness sake.' After removing Vargis's coat, she hurried away.

Jack, after pulling the iced-up balaclava from his head, kicked off his boots and went to the assistance of his father. He and Vargis escorted the shivering man into the kitchen. Mrs Evison watched them enter:

'Ruth will probably walk through the door in the morning as though nothing untoward has happened… Wonder what all the fuss was about.' She said, re-positioning a chair by the cooker. 'Bring him here where it's warm.'

Mr Evison, as if attempting to placate his wife, managed to walk the last few steps unaided. He slumped on the chair by the cooker, sighing deeply. A mug of hot tea was waiting for him on the cooker. He picked it up and wrapped his frozen fingers around the hot mug, raising it slowly to his lips, sipping cautiously. Jack and Mr Vargis sat up to the kitchen table and, after being furnished with a mug of hot tea apiece, they too warmed their hands in similar fashion. Mrs Evison reached inside a cabinet and took out a half-filled small bottle of rum. Vargis watching, licked his lips and focused upon the hand that drew the stopper from the bottle.

'A splash of rum, Mr Vargis?' Mrs Evison smiled,

pouring a measure of the dark liquid into his mug of tea before receiving his answer.

The gamekeeper smiled: 'I'm obliged to you, Mrs Evison.'

'It's I... We, who are indebted to you, Mr Vargis, for bringing my men home.'

'Well...'

'Mr Vargis said he saw Ruth and her friends in the forest this afternoon, mum.'

'Yes, yes I heard you the first time, Jack. And I wish he'd sent them home.'

Vargis cleared his throat: 'I did... Well... Thought I had; they set off in the direction of home. Blighters... Must have doubled back. Kids, huh, they'll take no notice of their elders these days, will they?' He said, slurping the fortified tea and sighing gratifyingly.

The kitchen fell silent for a while and all that could be heard was the wind howling and whistling as it passed around the farm buildings, only the mooing of a solitary cow intruding.

'I've some beef stew simmering,' Mrs Evison said suddenly.

'I'm starving,' said Jack.

'You'll have a dish of stew with us, won't you, Mr Vargis? A crust of bread?'

'I... I really ought to be heading back home...' The gamekeeper replied falteringly, refusing only out of politeness. He was cold and as hungry as anyone and would have died for a helping of Mrs Evison's stew. Licking his lips, he inhaled its hearty aroma and smiled.

'Of course he'll have some stew, mum.'

'Thank you, Mrs Evison,' the gamekeeper's smile widened. 'It'll save me the effort of making supper when I get back home.'

An entire white loaf was sliced and buttered and the slices thrown haphazardly onto a plate. Mrs Evison stirred the stew and then slid the pan from the heat, ladling it into the warmed dishes. Her husband, having sufficiently recovered, joined Jack and Vargis at the table, and a dish of steaming stew was set in front of each hungry man. Mrs Evison poured herself a mug of tea, topped up the men's mugs and then sat in the chair vacated by her husband. She watched the men eat and listened to them speaking animatedly of how their lives had been within inches of being wrestled from them.

In the warm convivial atmosphere of the kitchen it almost appeared that the plight of the children lost in the blizzard had been forgotten. But the night remained dangerous and intimidating and nothing more could be done except wait, hope and pray; wait until morning and hope that Ruth, Morton and Abigail had reached Blackdaw Cottage. Pray that each child would be found safe and well.

Vargis, after consuming supper, was anxious to return home, but after partaking of Mrs Evison's stew, he felt obliged to remain awhile and share their anxieties. Then the clock in the hall chimed eight times and he cleared his throat in readiness to announce his departure, when a frantic knock on the outer door accompanied by an equally frantic cry startled him. It startled them all.

CHAPTER 25

The pot, and pans and dishes had been washed and dried and put away in their rightful place; and the three children and their host, after feasting on the casseroled purloined pheasant, rested contentedly before the blazing fire with filled stomachs. Anyone passing by, glimpsing the tranquil scene, could be forgiven for thinking they had been transported back in time; to a distant age, to a life less complex uncluttered by the litter of modernity, when the days from dawn to dusk were occupied with the purpose of sustaining life. Time then was then precious, but a priceless portion was set aside for entertainment: games, songs and dancing; and stories were told from the memories of the family elders, tales of mystery, mutiny and murder, superstition and witchcraft. They were living stories, changing constantly to reflect the personality of the teller and the era in which they lived.

Elsa and Sputnik lay close to each other on the hearth, their ears alert to every sound inside or out; the wind's mournful howl, the logs crackling and spitting as they burned in the grate, to intermittent scratching in the rafters. Bentley ignored it all and appeared relaxed, his eyes were set wide, focusing on the flames crawling in a never-ending procession up the chimney breast. His arms, folded across his chest, rising and falling to the rhythm of his breathing – a twitching upper lip seemed to provide a beat.

What were his thoughts?

Trance-like, he shuffled to the edge of his seat, leaned forward and threw several logs onto the fire, before reclining with a sigh. His eyes maintaining the same abstracted intense stare.

What did he see? Vague images of a life, now consumed by the slavery of time! But is not all life enslaved? Progressing in a perpetual motion from the moment of creation until the end of time, mirroring the ripples of a shifting environment, evolving a little more with each generation into something incomprehensible? For life, all animate life, after mutating from the primeval slop, the slime that crawled ashore from the sea and spawned life, traverses along an infinite pathway, journeying to an unknown destination.

The warmth from the fire began to induce drowsiness, but it was much too early for bed, and excitable children imprisoned in a strange environment would surely find sleep elusive.

'Children, children!' Bentley said suddenly. 'What occupies your evenings when you are at home with your families?'

'I like to read stories,' Abigail said quickly.

'Stories!' Morton was aghast at the suggestion.

'What kind of stories?' Enquired Bentley.

'*Black Beauty* and *The Railway Children*.' She replied eagerly. '*Jane Eyre* and *Frankenstein*.'

'*Frankenstein*!' Morton said, glumly. 'I like to play out.'

'Well you can't play out tonight,' Abigail reminded him.

'No, no indeed, not,' agreed Bentley. 'But you, young man, must read also?'

'Reading's boring,' Morton declared.

Bentley chuckled: 'Aye, well, for boys maybe it is. Boys like to play outside, I expect. Climb trees, run about the parks and –'

'I read sometimes,' interrupted Ruth. 'But I like playing out best.'

'Yes, yes, and many times I've seen you and Morton

running about the fields, but you can't do that tonight. And I've nothing here to amuse children; no toys, no games, and no books for Abigail to read. So what are we to do?'

'You can tell us a story, you must know lots,' Abigail said.

'Must I indeed,' chuckled Bentley.

'Yes, you must,' agreed Morton, adding cheekily. 'Old people know lots of stories.'

'Old people!' Exclaimed Bentley, eyeing Morton irefully, before succumbing to thoughtfulness. 'Aye... You're right. I am old; and I know stories.' He said and fell silent, smiling abstractedly as he trawled the echelons of his brain, a brain slowed from the clutter accumulated from a long life. The children observed the firelight dancing upon his ruddy cheeks, his entire face; the light seemed to resurrect life to tired eyes, they widened and he smiled. 'Aye, I know stories, stories to chill your blood.'

'About cut throats and devils?' Morton, animated, was eager to know.

'Devils, aye!' Said Bentley, and with widening eyes he sprang forward abruptly, startling Morton. 'Murderers, madmen, and all kinds of wicked people.'

'People like Mrs Reed, the wicked aunt in *Jane Eyre*' Abigail asked.

'Mrs Reed!' Morton repeated contemptuously. 'That's silly girl's stuff. I don't want to hear stories about wicked aunts and Jane Eyre, they're nothing.'

'Nothing!' Chuckled Bentley. 'Well, I confess I know nothing of *Jane Eyre*, or wicked aunts. But I know a tale about a man and woman who lived in this very cottage many, many years ago.'

'A true story?' Enquired Morton.

'It must be true if it's about people who lived here,' supposed Ruth.

'Well, the truth is that no one knows for sure what is true and what isn't,' began Bentley. 'It happened such a long time ago and the tale has been told by many people over the years. People exaggerate, and fact and myth becomes confused –'

'Myth!' Morton interrupted.

'Aye, legend, imaginary tales of imaginary people or creatures like…' Bentley paused. 'Like Frankenstein, I suppose… Dracula. Stories embodying strange and unexplained phenomena.'

'But Frankenstein wasn't a real person!' Abigail said. 'You said your story was real and about real people.'

'Yes, yes,' laughed Bentley. The people are believed to have been real. Living at Blackdaw Cottage over two hundred and fifty years ago. But in those dark days few people could read or write – there was little writing paper or ink – and stories were not always written down. In those days stories were recited from memory, and tales told from memory alter a little each time – bits are forgotten, bits are invented.'

'You will tell us the story, won't you?' Asked Morton.

'Well… I'll see,' said Bentley, thoughtful and stroking his beard.

'But you must,' pleaded Abigail. 'Please say you will.'

Bentley remained thoughtful: 'Well… It's years since the story was told to me by my grandfather and I'm not sure how much of it I can remember.'

'Then you must make it up,' demanded Abigail. 'That's what you said other people did and you must do it also. But you must remember some of the story.'

'Aye, some I'll never forget,' said Bentley, again succumbing to thoughtfulness, a cheek, a lip convulsed and his features adopted a troubled expression. 'Some of it will remain with me until the day I die.' He spoke softly and slowly, staring straight ahead through unblinking eyes, as though memories he would rather forget had invaded his thoughts.

Abigail roused him: 'Please, please say you'll tell us the story, you must.'

'Must!' Uttered Bentley, momentarily disorientated and looking sharply to Abigail. 'Well, then maybe I will.'

'What was the man's name?' Ruth wished to know.

'Murdac.' Bentley said abruptly. 'The man's name was Ivan Murdac.'

'Ivan Murdac!' Repeated Morton, excitable and shuffling.

'Aye, and his wife, I believe, was called Gertrude.'

'I've heard their names before,' said Ruth. 'Old people whispering to other old people. But when I ask who they were, they say it's not for little girl's ears.'

'Not for little girl's ears!' Morton repeated. 'But you're not a little girl anymore, are you?'

'Well…' chuckled Bentley. 'Maybe I ought not talk of them either. Ivan, it was believed, was the devil and his wife a witch. But it's a horrible, terrible tale,' he said, looking at the serious faces of the children looking back at him through unblinking eyes. And then, for no apparent reason, the old man burst suddenly into laughter; loud uproarious laughter. The children were unsure whether to laugh with him, or flee the cottage and take their chance in the blizzard. With widening eyes they looked to each other, and then to Bentley before they too succumbed to laughter.

'Anyway Morton said you were the devil,' Abigail informed him.

'No, I did not,' protested Morton.

'Yes, you did. And you said you were going to burn his house down.' Abigail reminded him, turning to Ruth for support. 'Didn't he, Ruth? Didn't he say he was going to set fire to Blackdaw Cottage?'

Ruth compressed her lips and nodded.

'I did not,' Morton's protest grew louder.

'Children! Children!' Beseeched Bentley. 'Silence, if you please, or you might yet rouse the devil in me – awaken the curse of Murdac.'

'The curse of Murdac!' Queried Morton,

'Death to all who speak his name, or provoke his spirit.'

'We might all die if you tell the story!' Abigail presumed, starting when a persistent gust of wind shook the cottage to its foundations. It felt as though the frail building might collapse about them, leaving its inmates exposed to the mercy of the blizzard. The wind blew stronger and louder, culminating in an excruciating screech that sounded like a wounded animal in immense pain. The children gasped and looked anxiously to their protector.

Bentley smiled: 'The wind, the wind,' he chuckled. 'It's only the wind.'

'Maybe it'll blow the cottage down and we'll all freeze to death,' Morton said.

'But I don't want to die,' said Abigail, dismally.

'No one's going to die,' Bentley reassured them. 'Blackdaw Cottage has withstood worse, thunderstorms and hurricanes – fire.' He laughed.

'Once when I was naughty…' Morton began, sheepishly.

'Only once!' Interrupted Ruth, mocking.

Morton looked scornfully to her. 'Yes… Dad said the devil would come from the forest and take me away, but he didn't.' He blurted, bowing his head, looking nervously up towards Bentley and continuing in a whisper that was barely audible. 'And dad said you was the devil... Said you'd take me away and boil me in a big pot and...'

Bentley laughed, but a coughing fit curtailed his amusement. The old man's face turned crimson and his body convulsed. He began pounding his chest hard with both fists, gasping and coughing.

'Young man...' began Bentley, breathless. 'You mustn't make me laugh like that again. But let me tell you, had I been the devil, I'd have had you in my pot instead of the pheasant, long since.'

'Well, I knew you weren't really the devil,' Abigail said, slighted that the kindly old man could be thought capable of carrying out devilish deeds.

'Well, I... I knew as well,' said Morton, eager to dismiss the misconception impressed upon him through the prejudices of his father.

'Good, good,' chuckled Bentley. 'Then I'm sure we'll get along fine.'

'Did Mr Murdac murder people?' Asked Morton.

'Maybe, maybe not. Who knows! Evil acts were commonplace in those dark days, and victims had little recourse to justice. People then were a superstitious breed... Afraid of everything they didn't understand; witches, ghosts, demons and devils – they were even afraid of God. And honest, hardworking folk, struggling to raise children were wary of strangers, especially unsightly outcasts like the Murdacs.'

'But why were they afraid of the Murdacs?' Asked Abigail.

'Well... Ivan and Gertrude did not look particularly nice, and they didn't fit easily into society.' Bentley laughed. 'The same might be said about me. People then were suspicious of strangers, fearing they might be disciples of the devil, harbingers of disease. Nobody wanted the Murdacs near them and the pair was constantly driven from village to village, from town to town, and then they arrived at the place we now sit. Blackdaw Cottage; their last home on earth.'

'Then what happened to them?' Asked Morton.

'Terrible things,' said Bentley, shaking his head. 'Two poor souls alone in the wilderness, frightened out of their wits.' He lurched forward with lightning swiftness. 'And it'll frighten the life from you!'

The children gasped. Bentley reclined in his chair and broke into laughter. The horror that had gripped the children mutated slowly into smiles, into uninhibited laughter.

'It's a tale of spirits, wronged spirits taking revenge for Ivan's cruelty,' said Bentley, pointing to Elsa. 'A cat, a bonny white cat, like Elsa returned to haunt Murdac – the animal terrified them both.' He halted. 'Perhaps I shouldn't tell you the tale tonight. You'll not sleep a wink with the wind howling, and if you did you'd be troubled with nightmares.'

'But you promised,' said Abigail.

'Did I?' Chuckled Bentley.

'Yes, you did,' emphasised Ruth. 'Please, you must. You must tell the story, or what are we to do?'

'You could all go to bed!'

'But it's much too early for bed,' Abigail protested, to reinforcing cries of dismay from Ruth and Morton.

'Very well, children, very well.'

In truth, Bentley was as keen to tell the tale as the children were to hear it. What better way was there of unburdening himself of the age-old story than by bequeathing it to a new generation – instilling into the receptive minds of young children the tale of the Murdacs, where it might be preserved, nurtured and retold to future generations.

The excitement increased, and the three young adventurers shuffled in their seats; imaginations had been provoked and calm would not be restored until the story of Ivan and Gertrude Murdac, told by the present occupant of Blackdaw Cottage, had been revealed in all its terrifying detail. And what better way was there of rounding off an enjoyable evening than with a lively tale?

Since welcoming the children into his home (or was it the children who had welcomed him?) Bentley had so far successfully discharged all challenges put before him. Proving himself a competent cook, a caring guardian and now, potential entertainer. It was his wish was to make the children's visit to Blackdaw Cottage as memorable as he could, and the story of Ivan and Gertrude Murdac, he felt, would achieve this; implanting into impressionable minds a lasting memoir of the night the children strayed beyond sensible boundaries, during the worst snowstorm the country had witnessed in decades.

The children, should they survive the night, would be the next generation's keepers of the fable of Blackdaw Cottage. The tale retold, coloured by their own experiences, would reinvigorate the age-old story like never before; absorbing the dynamics of the shifting environment in which the storyteller and listener existed, until, like the dinosaurs, human life became extinct.

CHAPTER 26

Visitors had not been expected that night, given the atrocious weather. Mrs Evison turned to her husband and together they turned to Jack.

'I'll go,' he volunteered, rising to his feet and hurrying from the kitchen.

The thumping on the door became louder and a frantic male voice called out:

'Hello! Anyone there! Hello…!'

'All right, all right, I'm coming!' Jack called back. He turned the doorknob and opened the door. Snow was blown inside over him, and the snowdrift that had built up against the door toppled inside onto the doormat. The blizzard's wrath, though, was nothing compared to rancour of the irate male standing shivering on the doorstep with his wife. Their faces were obscured within the protective hoods of the pale-blue plastic mackintoshes they wore, but Jack recognised them. They were Abigail's parents, Mr and Mrs Markson.

'Listen here young man, I –'

'Clive!' The lady beseeched.

After glancing at the snow lying on the mat, Jack gestured to the visitors and invited them step inside. But Mr Markson was angry and anxious; their daughter had failed to return home and he was intent on attributing the blame to someone.

'Look here, young man, I want to know what –'

'Clive!' Mrs Markson again intervened.

'Please, step inside… Then I can close the door,' Jack urged. But the pair remained rooted where they stood, the thin plastic mackintoshes offering scant protection against the wind and snow. Their hems failed to cover the tops of their wellington boots, and the pair had walked some distance through knee-deep snow and much would have had fallen inside, chilling their feet.

Jack wiped the snow from his face and sighed. 'Please step inside,' he pleaded.

Mrs Markson grimaced and surged suddenly forward; she was eager to escape from the snow and the wind, but her husband thrust out an arm, preventing her from progressing further.

'Look here, young man, if you think –'

'Clive...!' Mrs Markson again interrupted, vociferously this time, as she glared at her husband. 'I'm frozen stiff standing here,' she protested, pushing his arm aside and stepping into the hall. Mr Markson was incensed and glared after her, but when a violent gust hurried him inside, he offered no resistance.

'Oh, very well,' he conceded grudgingly.

Jack bent down and scooped the snow up from the mat in his hands and threw it outside. He closed the door and turned to his visitors, but Mr Markson was waiting for him.

'Civility is well and good,' he said, eyeing Jack with unwarranted sternness. 'But I demand to know what you've done with our daughter?'

'Clive –!' Mrs Markson entreated. 'They've done nothing with Abigail... It's no fault of, of –'

'Jack.'

'It's not Jack's fault that Abigail and her friend's are lost in the snow.'

'Then whose –?'

Mrs Evison appeared in the hallway. 'Come on in Mrs Markson, Mr Markson,' she invited them. 'Bring them through into the kitchen, Jack, where it's warm. Don't keep them standing talking in the draughty hall. Take their coats first.'

Jack frowned and shook his head. He noticed Mrs Markson struggling to unfasten the pliable plastic buttons with fingers numbed from the cold and went to her aid, he took her coat and hung it on a hook behind the door.

'Take your wellingtons off, if you like,' Jack offered. 'They'll be full of snow, I expect.'

Mrs Markson smiled and removed her boots immediately. Her husband, standing watching, shook his head disapprovingly.

'Never mind about our boots, what about Abigail? What do you propose to do about her? That's what I want to know.'

Jack sighed. 'There's nothing you or anyone can do tonight, me and dad have –'

'If no one's prepared to go and look for our daughter, then I will,' interrupted Mr Markson, striding purposely towards the door, gripping the handle.

'Clive!' Mrs Markson implored. 'It would be foolish to –'

'Foolish! If you think searching in the snow for our daughter is foolish, then –'

'It'd be suicidal,' Jack intervened. 'Dad and me have already been out looking. We couldn't find them, so what chance you?'

'And where would you look, Clive?' Mrs Markson asked, screwing up her brow, eyeing her husband irefully. 'You wouldn't know were to start. Jack and Mr Evison know the area, you don't.'

Mr Markson retained his grip on the door handle and sighed protractedly.

'Me and dad were lucky,' Jack began. 'If it hadn't been for Mr Vargis, well –'

'Please, Clive,' Mrs Markson pleaded. 'You'd be lost in

the blizzard in no time at all. And then what use would you be to Abigail?'

The wind chose an opportune moment and gusted violently, as if to reinforce its threat. Mr Markson listened to its fury, sighed and then released the door handle.

'Oh, very well,' he conceded, tugging the plastic buttons apart. 'It's just so, so frustrating. I feel useless... Feel I've failed Abigail.' He removed the plastic mackintosh in the same belligerent manner that he dealt with the buttons, kicking off his wellington boots and abandoning them where they fell.

'Follow me,' said Jack.

The gamekeeper rose the instant Mr and Mrs Markson entered the kitchen, not out of politeness, but because he felt uncomfortable. He acknowledged the newly-arrived visitors with a tentative nod, and then cleared his throat, gesturing to Jack.

'I'll bid you goodnight, Jack... Mr and Mrs Evison, all of you.' Vargis said, as he shuffled past the visitors.

'Please don't leave on our account, Mr Vargis,' Mrs Markson blurted, smiling. Mr Markson turned sharply to his wife and glared.

'Stay the night, Mr Vargis!' Mrs Evison suggested. 'We've plenty of room.'

'I'm obliged to you, Mrs Evison, but I must return – dogs to feed.' Vargis replied, pulling the leather hat he held in his hands over his head, stepping nearer the door. 'I'll return first thing in the morning. With luck, the blizzard will have ceased. I'll show you the easiest way to Blackdaw Cottage.' He said, and then opened the door.

'Blackdaw Cottage!' Mrs Markson gulped. 'Isn't that where that, that –'

Vargis turned, but he spoke to Jack. 'And if you can get the tractor started, so much the better.'

'I'll do my best.'

'But the children!' Mrs Markson was alarmed and uneasy. 'Isn't Blackdaw Cottage the place where that awful tramp lives?'

'Well, that's it then!' Mr Markson interjected. 'If Abigail's at that evil den she must be brought home tonight. I'll go and fetch her myself if no one else will.'

'I'll bid you all goodnight,' said Vargis, hurrying from the kitchen.

'Wait!' Mr Markson beseeched. 'You know the way to –'

Vargis glanced briefly to him and then closed the door. Leaving Mr Markson stranded on the other side, staring in disbelief.

'But what about Abigail?'

'Abigail won't like it,' Mrs Markson said. 'Forced to sleep in the same house as that tramp. She won't like it at all.' She sniffed, and slumped in a chair by the table.

CHAPTER 27

Mr Markson sat in the chair at the side of his distraught wife, he placed a tentative hand on her shoulder, but gazed absently about; it was not until his eyes met Mrs Evison's that he felt compelled to draw his wife closer to him.

'The children will be fine,' Mrs Evison reassured the pair, even if she doubted the validity of her own words. 'Well, let's hope… They will be if they are at the cottage.'

'If!' Mr Markson stressed.

Mrs Markson, sniffing, faced her husband: 'Not since Abigail was a baby have I not been there to kiss her goodnight, have I Clive?'

'No, I don't suppose you have,' Mr Markson replied, somewhat reticently, relaxing his hold over his wife.

'The children will be fine, I'm sure,' Mr Evison said, reinforcing his wife's hopes. 'If they're in the cottage with old Bentley they'll be all right.'

'All right!' Mrs Markson exclaimed. 'Sleeping under the same roof as a… He might murder them as they sleep.'

The kettle began to sing.

'Let's have a cup of tea, shall we?' Mrs Evison said, turning her attention to the steaming kettle. 'We'll all feel better for a nice cup of tea.'

'A nice cup of tea!' Mr Markson repeated, sardonically.

'Come, come and sit by the cooker where it's warm,' Mrs Evison gestured.

'We're fine where we are, thank you.' Mrs Markson said.

Mr Markson sighed. 'My fault, I suppose?'

'It's no one's fault, Mr Markson,' Mrs Evison emphasised. 'Children… Well, they can't be watched every minute of every day.' She poured boiling water from the kettle into a large white teapot. 'We were no different when we were their age, were we? Didn't we always endeavour to learn everything the hard way?'

Mr Markson faced his wife. 'If I hadn't interfered, nay bullied you, Abigail would be at home, safe. Huh, so much for sledging! That's where she said she was going... Sledging with her friends. We were deceived, Lindsey – *I* was deceived.'

'I don't know that you were, Mr Markson,' Mrs Evison said. 'The children set out with good intentions; they took the sledge with them. Perhaps they got fed up dragging the sledge up the steep hill – got bored of sledging. Other ideas entered their heads, as happens with children – happens to all of us from time to time. No one expected the snow to arrive so soon, to fall as thick and fast. It took us all by surprise.'

'Huh, weather forecasters! Suited fortune-tellers, more like, posturing and smiling for the cameras,' mocked Mr Evison. 'What do they know? What do they get paid for? If they say it'll be sunny we get rain. Snow next week and we get it today. If we'd been better informed I'd have had the sheep down off the moors yesterday, long before all this blasted snow arrived.'

'Yes, yes,' Mr Markson conceded. 'Indeed it's much worse than I had believed, until I saw for myself – much worse.'

'Well, there you are,' Mr Evison said. 'Children are fascinated by the snow, and you can't stop them having fun... Can't keep them tethered up inside like cattle. They need an outlet for their energy... To find things out, discover things for themselves. They'll learn from their mistakes.'

'Three young children at the mercy of the blizzard!'

Scoffed Mr Markson. 'And goodness knows what else! It's indeed a harsh lesson.' He concluded, shaking his head before continuing. 'When we lived in the city we seldom dare let Abigail from our sight. The place these days is teeming with unsavoury characters, pickpockets and vagabonds. We thought we would be safer in the country. We thought Abigail would be safe.'

'And she would be, if it wasn't for the unusually heavy snowfall,' Mrs Evison said; she forced a smile. 'But she will be, and when summer's here, you'll be glad… You'll see then that you made the right decision.' She shuffled mugs into a line, poured out tea and handed a mug each to their guests. 'They'll be having the time of their lives – they will, if I know our Ruth. Help yourselves to milk and sugar.'

Mrs Markson reached for the sugar bowl and spooned two spoonfuls of the white crystals into her husband's tea, adding a splash of milk into both mugs and stirring.

'We tried to phone earlier but the lines must be down,' Mrs Markson said.

'Our phone is fine,' Mrs Evison informed her. 'Or it was a few minutes ago.' She stepped to the kitchen cabinet, raised herself on tiptoe, reached inside and lifted out a cake tin. She set the tin down on the table and prised off the lid. 'Scones anyone? I'm famished – fit to faint if I don't eat something soon.' She carried the butter dish, a large floral plate and a stack of side plates to the table. She procured a glass and silver condiment set which, after setting it down, lifted the silver lids from the two glass vessels and pushed the two silver spoons into the bejewelled burgundy jams. Scones were dissected and buttered and the halves arranged on the floral plate. 'Help yourselves,' Mrs Evison offered, shuffling a side plate in front of each guest. 'There's damson, and cherry – both home-made.'

'Thank you, Mrs Evison, the scones look absolutely delicious, as does your jam, but I'm afraid I've little appetite right now.' Mrs Markson said, eyeing the scones, fingering the raised pattern on the glass vessel.

'You should eat something, Lindsey,' urged Mrs Evison, adding swiftly. 'I won't be offended if you can't eat up. I find a morsel of sweet food reviving in a time of crisis.'

'Mm…' Mrs Markson murmured, after sipping tea. She set the mug down on the table. 'Perhaps I will try one,' she said, picking up a scone and placing it on a plate. Using a silver spoon, she scooped out a large globule of damson jam and unloaded it onto the scone, levelling the gummy preserve with the back of the spoon. 'Mm.' She uttered, after biting into the scone, brushing the crumbs from her lips with her fingertips. 'Are you having one, Clive? Mrs Evison's damson jam is absolutely delicious.'

Mrs Evison poured tea into a further three mugs – for herself, her husband and Jack – before sitting at the table; and all partook of the home-made scones and home-made jams, even Mr Markson, and Mrs Markson felt compelled to sample the cherry jam also.

'Listen to the wind, Clive!' Mrs Markson commented, as she ate. 'We've yet to step back out into it.'

'Stay the night!' Mrs Evison said. 'You must.' She insisted. 'We've rooms to spare, and there's no sense traipsing back out tonight through all that snow.'

'Thank you, Mrs Evison but we really couldn't impose,' Mrs Markson replied.

'Impose! Nonsense.' Mrs Evison turned to her husband for support. 'They must stay, mustn't they?'

'Aye…'

'It's kind of you, but we've got nothing with us – our things.'

'*Things*!' Mrs Evison responded. 'What *things* do you

need for a good night's sleep for goodness sake? We've spare pyjamas.'

'If you stay, Clive'll be at hand in the morning,' Mr Evison said. 'I presume you will be joining us when we go out looking for the children?'

'Well, I…' Mr Markson turned to his wife: she smiled and nodded. 'Yes, yes I'd like to if you think I can be of use?'

'And Abigail will be pleased if…' Mrs Markson began, but she halted mid-sentence and her hands flew up to her face. 'What if Abigail returns and we're here?'

'The children will be going nowhere tonight,' Mr Evison assured her.

He was probably right; no one with an iota of common sense would step out while the blizzard raged thus. It was bitterly cold, and visibility in the swirling snow was almost zero. The five adults, sitting in the kitchen, remained ponderous and anxious, listening to the wind, when the telephone in the hall rang, rousing them from indulgent thought. Its ring sounded loud, its tone urgent.

'News of the children!' Mrs Markson dared to think out aloud, animated and turning to her husband. He did not share her optimism and her excitement abated; heads all turned and eyes focused upon Mrs Evison hurrying towards the door. She disappeared into the hall and the ringing fell silent.

'Hello… Yes, yes… That's right.' The tone of her voice was at first firm and clear, but then it quietened and adopted a note of sadness. 'Oh, no, dear me, no!'

The sitters in the kitchen remained silent, their gazes flitting fitfully from one to the other. Mrs Evison continued:

'… But that… That's dreadful. Terrible! Dear, dear, poor Morton. How awful… Yes, yes, indeed it is. And what –?'

'Morton… What!' Mrs Markson blurted, staring across the table to Mr Evison.

'Who is it?' Mr Evison called out.

His wife's conversation continued with whomever was on the other end of the line. 'No, no, my husband and Jack went out earlier… Almost got themselves killed.' She paused. 'It's bad, very bad. And the snow's falling still… No, of course not, no. All we can do is wait, hope and pray.' She paused. 'Yes, yes, if the snow stops falling, the men are hoping to go to Blackdaw Cottage in the morning. Mr Vargis thinks the children might be at the cottage.'

The receiver was parked in its cradle, the floorboards in the hall creaked and Mrs Evison reappeared in the kitchen. 'Oh, dear!' She mumbled, closing the door.

'Well, what is it?' Mr Evison asked, his eyes following his wife as she trod solemnly towards the chair by the cooker. Sighing deeply and sitting before speaking.

'Poor Morton. That was the police.'

'The police!' Gasped Mrs Markson. 'What! Morton… Dead!'

'No, no, no.'

'What's happened to Morton then?'

'Nothing's happened to Morton. Well… Not that we know of. It's Morton's dad, poor man. Morton's dad has been found dead at the wheel of his car. Froze to death, the police said.'

'Morton's dad! Dead!' Mr Markson gasped. 'I'm sorry –'

'Poor Morton,' repeated Mrs Evison, shaking her head. 'The police said Mr Rymer was probably knocked unconscious when his car skidded off the road. This horrid, weather, I'll be glad to see the back of it. Lost control on the ice, that's what the police think… Hit a wall and turned upside down in a ditch. Hypothermia, the policeman thought. If it hadn't been for this blizzard…'

If an adult, protected from the worst extremes of the weather inside the protective shell of a motor car was unable to remain alive, what hope for the children? And even if they were at Blackdaw Cottage, the fragile building is situated in a clearing in the forest, exposed to all kinds of weather. The dilapidated cottage would be like a magnet to the spiteful frost. Granting easy access through its crumbling walls and, once inside, the cruel frost would seek out those inside, sneak into their marrow of their bones and snuff out life as they slept.

'What will the boy do now?' Mr Evison asked, looking to his wife.

'Morton will come and stay with us, that's what.' Mrs Evison was decisive. 'He'll be fine with us, given the circumstances. Morton always enjoys playing on the farm with Ruth.'

'But what of Morton's mother?' Mrs Markson enquired.

'She left home some time ago,' Mrs Evison informed her.

'What! Abandoned the poor boy?' Mrs Markson was exasperated. 'Well, what kind of a mother!'

'She wanted to take Morton with her,' Mrs Evison went on. 'But he wouldn't be parted from his friends – wouldn't leave Ruth. So he remained in the village with his dad.'

'He hated liked living with his dad though,' Jack said. 'His dad was a drunk; a bully and –'

'Jack!' Mr Evison snapped. 'You shouldn't speak ill of the dead.'

'But it's true, he –'

'Jack…!'

News of anyone's death comes as a shock, regardless of their morals or character; whether they were good or bad human beings. But death is an inevitability from which no one will escape, and its presence focuses minds, provokes the living to reflect upon the fragility of life and consider their own mortality.

An early night now beckoned even though it had not long turned eight o'clock. But who would find sleep while vulnerable children remained lost in the blizzard? It was destined to be another extremely cold night, and once the snow had ceased to fall and the frosts became established, all England shivered on that tempestuous December night.

CHAPTER 28

Inside the cottage in the forest, life was much less fraught; it was warm and cosy, even though the fire began to burn low. Ordinarily at this hour on such a cold night, alone with his cat, Bentley would have retired to his bed. But tonight was no ordinary night, and Bentley was not alone. He rose from his chair, piled the remaining logs from the hearth onto the fire, perched on the edge of his chair, kicked off his slippers and pulled on his wellington boots.

'Need more logs,' he uttered, standing and stepping towards the door, unhooking a coat from the nail behind the door and putting it on. 'Stay put by the fire, children,' he bid them. He unlatched the door, picked up a shovel and stepped outside into deep snow, closing the door behind him. He knew where the woodshed stood, but could see only a blurred image of it through the falling snow, even though it was only a dozen strides away. He immediately began shovelling the snow aside, opening up a pathway to the woodshed.

After some minutes of toil, he achieved his objective, pushed open the shed door and entered. Right of the entrance, logs were stacked up to the roof, but Bentley turned left and stepped to a door that was ajar. He poked his head inside and passed a cursory inspection, before walking to the woodpile where he loaded his arms with logs.

Back inside the cottage all remained calm. Sputnik was stretched regally on the floor alongside his feline companion. When Ruth reached out and stroked him, the dog's eyelids flipped open; he yawned and stretched and beat the floor with his tail. Morton, sitting motionless in his chair with his arms folded across his chest, glanced intermittently to the door with growing impatience; he looked to Ruth and to Abigail.

'I wish he'd hurry up,' he said, with a sigh.

The words had barely left his lips when the door flew open and logs falling to the floor startled him. Gasping aloud, Morton turned to the whitened figure entering.

'The door, if you please, the door,' laughed the shivering snowman. Ruth was the quickest off the mark. 'Good girl, good girl… Shut out the cold,' he said, stamping his feet on the floor to dislodge the snow from his boots. As Bentley hastened towards the fire with the logs, Sputnik raced past him to Ruth. The dog eyed the closed door, before turning to Ruth, whining.

'What's the matter, Sputnik?' She asked. 'A wee, is that what you want?'

Bentley unloaded the logs; or rather the logs fell from his arms and scattered about the hearth, causing Elsa to jump up and leap aside. He retrieved the spilt logs from the entrance.

'Put a coat over your shoulders if you're taking your dog outside,' Bentley said to Ruth. 'There's a closet in the woodshed if anyone needs it – I've cleared a path.' After tidying up the logs, stacking several more onto the fire, he sat and warmed his feet before putting on his slippers. 'I've not seen snow fall like it in years.' He said, chuckling softly. 'I was a young man then, a strong man and my bones could tolerate the cold – they can't anymore.'

Ruth took a coat from behind the door and spread it over her shoulders; and the instant she opened the door, Sputnik raced outside. Ruth followed and closed the door.

It had turned eight-thirty by the time the children, either out of curiosity or from necessity, had visited the woodshed, and were comfortable in front of the roaring fire. In the forest and beyond, the snow continued to fall, it drifted high around the four walls of the cottage, enclosing it slowly in a cold white cocoon. In open fields, snow lay on the ground at a level depth of eight, ten, even twelve inches, but deeper, much deeper where the wind had applied its mischief. Walls, fences and hedges were buried from sight and in places snowdrifts stood taller than the tallest man. Fortune had so far been kind to the three adventurers; without the shelter of Blackdaw Cottage and its caring guardian, the children, alone in the wilderness, would have struggled to remain alive.

The kettle boiled and Bentley removed it from the heat, carrying it to the stone slab by the sink. He poured boiling water into a jug, and the jug was set on a wooden tray with three mugs. A cake tin was procured and opened – the lid dropped onto the floor and retrieved – and chunks of parkin, moist spicy ginger cake, were arranged on a plate and the plate was placed on the tray. The old man picked up the tray and carried it to the impatient children.

'Is that gingerbread?' Asked Abigail, noticing a plate piled high with the light brown squares.

'You're not far wrong, bonny girl. Its parkin; baked this morning before daybreak to my grandmother's recipe.'

'What's in the jug?' Asked Morton, craning his neck in order to see inside when Bentley lowered the tray onto the table in front of them. 'It smells like, like –'

'Like orange juice, I hope,' Bentley intervened, chuckling.

'Hot orange juice!' Exclaimed Morton, frowning.

'Aye, hot orange juice,' Bentley repeated, lifting the jug from the tray, filling the three mugs with juice. 'This'll warm your bellies.'

'Hot orange juice!' Abigail remarked. 'It sounds

horrible. I don't know if I should like hot orange juice.'

'Try it and see,' Bentley bid her, handing her a mug. 'And if hot orange cordial's not to madam's liking, madam must say what she desires and I'll do my best to procure whatever drink the finicky young lady desires.'

Morton wasted little time, helping himself to the largest square of parkin he could find, biting eagerly into it. Ruth was thirsty and lifted a mug of juice up to her nose; she inhaled its vapours, before sipping tentatively. Frowning, she licked her lips, but quickly took a second sip and smiled. Morton, observing her, picked up a mug and was about to drink when he spotted a worrying anomaly.

'Why are there only three pots!'

'Whisky,' uttered Bentley, hastening towards the cabinet, chuckling. 'Whisky for me.'

Abigail, after observing Ruth's approving smile, picked up a mug and tasted the juice for herself. The hot orange cordial was a new experience, and at first she thought the taste strange. The anticipated sweetness from the oranges were subordinated to a bitter tang, but she licked her lips and took another sip. Bentley, returning with the whisky and glass tumbler, saw the smile on Abigail's lips; the delight and animation on each of the children's faces as they partook of the delicacies before them. He sat down, drew the stopper from the bottle and poured a measure of whisky into the glass tumbler.

'May the Lord keep us safe.' He said, lifting the glass to his lips and sipping.

'Can we have some whisky?' Asked Morton.

'You may not, young man.'

'Why not?'

'Whisky is a man's medicine.' He said, sipping some more. 'A-h-h... That'll put a fire in my belly – keep me alive throughout the cold night.'

'But what are we to have to keep us alive?' Asked Abigail.

Bentley laughed: 'Young children need of no warming spirits to keep their hearts beating,' he said, pouring himself another whisky.

'You'll get drunk,' warned Morton. 'And then you won't be able to remember the story. When my dad gets drunk he can't speak properly and –'

'Better put it away then,' said Bentley, setting the tumbler down on the floor, pushing the cork stopper back into the bottle.

Parkin and hot orange cordial seemed an odd combination; the sweetness of the parkin exaggerated the bitterness of the orange juice. But freshly baked parkin, eaten while the outer layer remained crunchy, and the centre soft and moist, taken with a mug of warming juice, was a treasured treat that Bentley had enjoyed at the home of his grandparents during school holidays on cold winter nights. The same combination, enjoyed by his three young guests, seemed as pleasurable to the children has it had been to him, all those years ago. Bentley hoped that they might one day introduce the same combination to children of their own – to their grandchildren.

'Right children,' began Bentley, shuffling. 'Time for the story.'

Eager eyes turned and focused on the elderly gentleman, and Bentley's timing proved fortuitous for the wind, as if articulating its own impatience, gusted hard and long. Its droning howl culminating in a chilling screech that caused the children to sit up and stare through widening eyes.

CHAPTER 29

The children, seated in an arc left of the fire – Morton the furthest from it, Abigail closest with Ruth nestling between – looked eagerly to the old man sitting opposite. Bentley cleared his throat, and the story of Ivan and Gertrude Murdac began…

'Night was falling fast and two weary travellers, Ivan and Gertrude Murdac, looked up to the lightning that zigzagged across the sky; thunder followed, rumbling threateningly in the distance. Gertrude, cradling a white cat in her arms, turned to her husband:

'"We must find a place quickly where we can shelter from the storm. Villages and towns must be close by."

'Ivan shook his head and laughed sardonically. "What town, what village will accommodate us? People everywhere despise us. They'll drive us away the instant they set eyes on us."

'He was right; the Murdacs were outcasts, and no one wanted them in their community. Ivan knew it and Gertrude knew it. Everywhere they went they encountered the same hostile reception. In every town and village they entered they were met by angry mobs and driven away.

'Exhausted and hungry, the pair limped on along a stony track in shoes that were worn through. They prayed they might stumble on a building where they could shelter for the night. But winter was approaching fast and one night's shelter was of little use, they needed somewhere where they could set up home and live throughout the desolate winter months.

'Rain teemed upon them from the sky, and it was pitch black when they entered a forest – their path lit only by sporadic bursts of lightning. Ivan hoped they might find hedges or holly bushes under which they could shelter from the rain, but he could find nothing other than sycamore trees, elm and ash. Onward the pair trudged through the dark, wet woodland, fighting their way beneath low lying branches, stumbling into trees and becoming entangled in brambles. Ivan yelled out, cursing his ill luck when pine needles stung his eyes, but rage turned rapidly to exaltation.

'"Stay close, wife," he bid Gertrude, gleeful and laughing.

'She took hold of his coat and clung on, as Ivan led her into a thicket of densely planted pine trees. He selected a mature tree with a thick trunk, laden with downward-sloping branches, knowing that the ground at its base would be dry – the frond-like branches having deflected the rain. He was right, the ground around its trunk was dry; it was spongy from the layers of fallen pine needles, forming the perfect bed on which the Murdacs could lie down on for the night.

'Wet and exhausted, the weary travellers bedded down quickly, huddling together for warmth beneath animal skins that Ivan carried with him. Soon they were fast asleep, with Gertrude's cat, Snowflash, lying in the hollow between them, purring contentedly.

'When Ivan next awoke it was midday; the sky was clear and the sun's dappled rays, projecting warm light through the gently swaying branches, dazzled him. Stretching and yawning, he meandered from beneath the trees and into a clearing, eagerly scanning the forest far beyond the fringes of pines, where drifts of oak, elm, ash and sycamore were dominant. An object glinting in the sunlight caught his eye. Squinting hard, he struggled to make out what it was, and when a cloud closed out the sun, Ivan's heart jumped. Yelling Gertrude's name, he raced back to the place he had left her.

'"A home, wife, I've found us a home!" Ivan felt certain that the object reflecting the sunlight was glass – a window set in a building, he hoped. Animated, the pair gathered together their meagre belongings, bundled them up and set out full of optimism, hardly daring to hope that Ivan might be proved right.

'Ivan was right. After walking for more than an hour their spirits were lifted when they came upon a dilapidated building. The windows were broken, slates were missing from the roof, the walls were crumbling and full of holes where jackdaws flew in and out, but the pair was not disheartened.

'The birds, agitated by the presence of strangers, flew frantically about, cawing and squawking. Their animation heightened when Ivan kicked down the rotten door and entered. Rats scurried everywhere, along the floor and up the walls, but Gertrude did not flinch. She was happy and cared little about the rats, the jackdaws or the dilapidated state of the building. The pair rejoiced and celebrated their good fortune with a jig, jumping and hugging, cheering and laughing.

'Ivan set immediately to work, clearing out the debris where the rats and jackdaws had made their nests. He toiled hard and fast for days, beginning at daybreak and working until darkness fell – sometimes after. He fixed the roof, the walls and fashioned new window frames from tree branches with an axe, and fixed them into position. A door was made and hung, and all that was needed was glass to shut out the jackdaws – the rats had already fled.

'One night after dark, Ivan set out for the nearby village, and from a greenhouse he stole all the glass he needed and carried it back to the cottage. Within weeks,

Ivan had transformed the ruin; he and Gertrude had a home of their own, but the jackdaws had lost theirs. The bewildered birds flew into the glass panes; they pecked the glass. Distraught and angry at being unable to enter, the jackdaws roosted in the trees; perched on the roof and cawed day and night. The noise drove Ivan crazy. He tried to train Snowflash to chase them away, but the cat had grown lazy from the years of pampering and the birds had little to fear.

'Ivan was tall and muscular, narrow dark eyes were set deep beneath a wrinkled brow. His black hair was long and unkempt; his beard matted and threaded with white streaks. His speech was abrupt and, when angry, resembled little more than an unintelligible grunt. Gertrude, by comparison, was tiny; but she could have been mistaken for Ivan's sister instead of his wife. Her nose protruded through a mass of dark hair that hung about her face; her pale skin made her lips appear unnaturally vibrant. She appeared nervous and piercing eyes searched constantly, her ragged dress danced about her thin legs, mirroring her uneasy gait. Snowflash was a dishevelled thing with ragged ears, but the cat kept her white coat white pristine. Gertrude favoured Snowflash over her husband and, unsurprisingly, Ivan detested the animal. When the animal was not sleeping she was eating.

'"Useless, scrawny animal!" Ivan had yelled, when the cat refused to chase away the jackdaws. In a rage, he chased after the birds himself, lashing out with his feet, hurling sticks and stones at them, but the jackdaws kept returning, flying about his head, showering him with droppings.

'Winter changed everything. Weeks of hard frosts turned the ground to iron, food became impossible to find and the pair at Blackdaw Cottage was starving slowly to death. Out of desperation, Ivan one day fastened their last morsel of food to the ground, fixing over it a wooden box propped up on a stick attached to a length of string. Hidden from view, Ivan sat holding tight to the other end of the string, watching and waiting. The temptation of food proved irresistible to the hungry jackdaws. The birds flew down from the roof and trees, stepping unwittingly beneath the trap to get at the food. Ivan waited patiently until several jackdaws were beneath the box, and then yanked the string hard. The stick shot out and the box fell over the jackdaws, trapping several beneath it. Excited and jubilant, Ivan ran to the box, eased it up and reached inside, dragging out two squawking jackdaws. After wringing their necks, he plucked the birds outside the cottage, drew out their intestines and flung them at their noisy cousins.

'"Feast on that, vermin," yelled Ivan, laughing crazily.

'Gertrude that night lit a fire and cooked the jackdaws in a pot with their last remaining rotting vegetables, and the pair feasted on meat for the first time in weeks.

'The Murdacs, though rough and strange, were neither beggars nor thieves; all they wished for was to be given a chance. Ivan sought work, and it was his abiding wish to be employed and provide for his wife like any other man, but no one would employ him. Gertrude longed to be settled, to be given the chance to live a normal life; to have children and enjoy the company of friends and neighbours, but no one wanted to know them. Once discovered, their presence caused pandemonium. Panic-stricken parents, armed with sticks and knives, gathered in the streets and drove them away.

'But no one knew of the Murdacs presence at Blackdaw Cottage until the gamekeeper one day saw smoke rising from the chimney. He hid in some shrubbery, watched and waited until a man appeared carrying a pheasant, walking with it to the very place we now sit...'

At that juncture in the story Bentley paused. He glanced to the children, picked up the glass tumbler from the floor and swallowed a draught of whisky.

'Was the gamekeeper Vargis?' Asked Morton.

'No, no,' the storyteller chuckled. 'The tale is two hundred and fifty years old. Vargis is an old fool, but he's not that old. No, I've no recollection of the gamekeeper's name.' He leant forward, built up the fire before reclining back in his chair, sipping more whisky. The children took the opportunity to top up their mugs with the cooling orange cordial and drink some more. Then Bentley set the tumbler back down on the floor, and the story of Ivan and Gertrude Murdac continued...

'...Right, where was I...? Ah, yes... The gamekeeper. Well, the gamekeeper was rightly incensed seeing a stranger stealing his pheasants, and Vargis, as you children well know, would be furious if he saw you or I carrying off one of his pheasants. Well, the gamekeeper contemplated how best to retrieve the bird without endangering his own life. And then Ivan called out:

'"Gertrude!" He shouted her name repeatedly until she appeared in the doorway. Her ashen face was expressionless, but then she saw the pheasant Ivan held up. Shrieking her delight, she ran barefoot from the cottage up to him, threw her arms around his neck and kissed his cheeks and his lips. A stick on which the gamekeeper stepped snapped, Gertrude turned her head sharply in his direction and her keen eyes looked out through the tangle of black hair, searching. The gamekeeper remained motionless in the bushes, hardly daring to draw breath and Gertrude, seeing nothing, turned her attention to the pheasant, examining it with her bony fingers. Overcome with joy, she again embraced her husband, kissing him fervently again and again.

'"Oh, Murdac, now we can eat meat, good, fresh meat," she enthused. Ivan, delighting in her kisses, allowed the arm that held the pheasant to relax and the bird hung low at his side. While distracted, Snowflash crept stealthily towards them, rising up on her hind legs and grasping the pheasant in her claws and jaws, attempting to wrestle it from Ivan's grip.

'"Scram, scrawny wretch," he hollered, his face twisting with rage, as he kicked out. "Scram moggy or I'll skin you alive, damn you." Snowflash had grown wise to his cruelty and lurched from his reach. "Go, wretch. Go catch food for yourself, or by God I'll make food of you."

'Gertrude eyed Ivan with contempt. She freed herself, bent and lifted Snowflash up from the ground. "You poor thing," she said, comforting the purring animal.

'"You spoil that darn thing," raged Ivan. "Teach it to chase the jackdaws away, catch food for herself, lazy, useless cat!" He hollered, inching his way towards his wife; his left cheek twitching. Gertrude backed away, matching him step for step, before turning and fleeing into the cottage.

'The instant she turned, the gamekeeper noticed her swollen stomach: Gertrude was to have a baby. Though the gamekeeper despised Ivan for stealing the pheasant, he pitied Gertrude and decided to leave them alone, vowing to himself to keep secret the presence of the Murdacs at Blackdaw Cottage.

'But winter compromised that promise. Heavy snowfalls, followed by weeks of keen frosts, rendered life at the cottage unbearable. The rabbits that the pair had relied on for sustenance had either died, or had taken up refuge in their underground burrows. The pheasants had disappeared and all they had to eat were the stiffened carcass of carrion scavenged from beneath the snow. Ivan was forced to take greater risks; he trespassed on the surrounding farms and stole eggs from the hen houses, and when the chickens stopped laying, he carried away the birds – always careful to brush away his footprints with tree branches on retreating.

'The farmers scratched their heads, unable to first understand why the chickens produced no eggs, or to where the birds later disappeared. Foxes were suspected, but they saw no paw-prints in the snow. Then one day, a sheep was discovered with its throat slit, its hind legs torn from its body, its loin, liver and kidneys removed – Ivan would have taken the whole animal had it not been too heavy to carry back to the cottage – but he left vital evidence behind. The farmers were in uproar, and gamekeeper was forced to reveal his knowledge of the Murdacs at Blackdaw Cottage. The villagers were outraged, demanding he go there and drive the interlopers away. The gamekeeper agreed, if someone would accompany him, but no one would. All were afraid that their actions might awaken the plague – the plague that was rumoured to strike wherever Ivan and Gertrude had settled in the past. Thus far no child had died; and so it was decided if the Murdacs were left alone the plague might pass them by.

'But when neither Ivan nor Gertrude had been seen for days, the gamekeeper feared his instincts might be proved right – that the plague had struck. He maintained a daily vigil over the cottage, but was reluctant to step too close from fear of being struck down with illness. The weather was particularly bad at the time; thunderstorms raged and hailstones battered the homes in the village. Snow fell heavily and temperatures plummeted below zero, remaining there throughout the day. Coughs and colds were commonplace, but when the plague struck and children began to die, fingers were pointed to the pair at Blackdaw Cottage.

'Several weeks passed before the gamekeeper next saw Ivan. He was emaciated; his body was bent and he limped about the forest, cradling his head in his hands, cursing and growling. Halting periodically, looking about and listening, before setting off again in a rage, pummelling the sides of his head with his fists. One day, when a crow fell from a tree a short distance away, Ivan raced to the spot where the bird had fallen, but he was beaten to it by a swarm of rats. Feathers flew in the frenzy, and when Ivan reached the bird all that remained was a spattering of feathers and a crimson patch on the snow. Enraged and yelling, he charged into the writhing, squealing mass, kicking out; rats were lifted into the air by Ivan's boot, others scurried away, and when the infestation had dispersed several lay lifeless on the ground. Anger turned to jubilation; Ivan gathered up the rats and carried them away by their tails, laughing maniacally. That night, Gertrude cooked the rats in a pot with spices, herbs and berries they had stored beneath the snow.

'Unknown to the Murdacs, trouble was brewing in the village. Parents and grandparents were distraught and angry; their children were dying and they demanded vengeance. Something had to be done or soon, they knew, or there would be no child left alive in the village.

'The couple at the cottage grew healthier and fatter, Ivan grew straight and his limp was miraculously cured. And the gamekeeper! He disappeared some weeks earlier and was never seen or heard of again…

'Spring arrived and the children continued to perish. One wet day, an anguished man and his distraught wife watched as the coffin of their daughter was lowered into the earth in the churchyard. Her grave was sealed and the girl's father, Gabriel Mayhew, dried his tears, he became angry. Trouble would soon afflict the lives of Ivan and Gertrude Murdac.

CHAPTER 30

'One day in May, Ivan and Gertrude sat enjoying the late afternoon sunshine outside their cottage. He was relaxed and calm, no longer the cursing, bullying brute and looked forward to fatherhood, fussing continually over Gertrude, attending to her every need.

'As evening approached, the atmosphere turned heavy and sticky, mists descended, thickening and fusing with other mists. Black clouds rolled across the sky, the day darkened and everything became hushed and still.

'Then a breeze dispersed the mists and agitated the grasses; it blew stronger and colder, the leaves on the trees trembled, as if the unseen hands of giants had gripped their trunks and shook them. Ivan stared into the forest, searching for the force that could not be seen. Birds were enlivened, startling him with their squawking, as they darted from tree to bush and back, as though pursued by a hungry hawk. Lightning flashed across the sky, and the deafening explosion of thunder that followed shook the earth. Forest animals – deer, rabbits, squirrels, mice and rats – scurried aimlessly about. All were searching for safety, but safety from what? Then, within seconds, the bright spring evening had turned blacker than midnight, and for one terrifying moment Ivan and Gertrude thought that they had been struck blind, but a lightning strike reassured them they were not.

'The storm grew fiercer and lightning ripped the angry black clouds apart; fire spewed from the widening fissure, sucking the oxygen from the air. Ivan and Gertrude, gasping and choking, felt that they would breathe their last breaths when the clouds released the rain, bringing instant relief. Gertrude stood petrified, looking to her husband for an explanation: he could provide none. He stepped to her side, gathered her in his arms and guided her into the cottage, but the cottage was no longer a safe refuge. Rain and hail, energised by the wind, battered the frail building, windows were broken and slates were dislodged from the roof and crashed to the ground.

'Ivan observed as Gertrude's fingers soothed the bulge that was their unborn child. His mood darkened suddenly, a cheek twitched, his brow furrowed and he turned from her and strode angrily to the window, where he stood, staring out at the descending white mists that gyrated in the sky. He watched as the mesmerising clouds loomed closer, churning with dizzyingly speed and forming an image recognisable to him – Gertrude's dead cat, Snowflash.

'"Damn you!" Ivan roared. The apparition, weeping tears of blood, filled the entire window with its menacing form. Gertrude saw it.

'"Snowflash…!" She called out. "Wasn't me…Wasn't me that strangled –"

'"Silence, damn you!" Ivan yelled.

'The pair stood for a while, transfixed and watching as the feline's mouth stretched wider. When it seemed it might swallow them, and the entire cottage, a chilling cry erupted, which provoked a reciprocal response from Gertrude. But her pain was real; Ivan knew it and he guided her into the next room where he lowered her onto a bed. Leaving her, he returned to the next room and stepped back up to the window. The image was waiting and greeted him with a terrific cry that chilled his blood.

'"Let me be, beast," pleaded Ivan. But he remembered, he remembered his cruelty; he remembered his own pain as the cat, in her desperate fight for life, sunk her claws deep into his flesh. Snowflash was no match for his brutality though, and the animal's best efforts could not prevent his hands from strangling the life from Gertrude's beloved cat. He and Gertrude had been unwell, they were starving to death and Ivan saw only one solution. Snowflash must be sacrificed in order that they might live: the evil deed he knew was wrong…

'Through the thunder, Ivan heard Gertrude's screams pitch higher and wilder. The apparition wailed; lightning flashed and the thunder crashed and when Ivan's brain could withstand the torment no more, he locked his hands over his ears, screwed his eyes tight and roared like a lion. On re-opening his eyes, he glanced into the adjoining room and saw Gertrude sat upright on her bed, cradling a child in her arms. Amidst the confusion and commotion, their child had been born.

'Gertrude rocked back and forth, humming a lullaby, but the infant failed to respond, remaining silent and still. The apparition at the window appeared jubilant, and Ivan, consumed with rage, seized hold of a chair and, wide-eyed and yelling, hurled it at the mocking phantom. The window exploded, banishing the image of Snowflash, allowing rain and hail to pour inside. Ivan turned to his wife and saw for the first time the fullness of the hideous infant in her arms.

'"Son of the devil!" He roared, turning when lightning struck outside the window, slamming fire into a tree. The tree shuddered and swayed; it illuminated from its base to the tips of its uppermost branches, as flaming bark exploded from its trunk. Ivan turned from the spectacle and stepped to his wife's bedside, he reached out, but when Gertrude felt his cold hand, she recoiled. She despised him for his false sympathy and beat him away with her fists.

'"Get from me, brute!" She screamed, looking upon the child on her lap. "This, Murdac, is your doing! Vengeance for your vile deeds."

'Ivan stepped from her; he filled a beaker with water from an enamelled jug sat in an enamelled basin on a cabinet. Returning with the water, he gesticulated; Gertrude eyed him with contempt, but when he put the mug to her parched lips she snatched hold of the vessel and gulped like a desert nomad, delirious after travelling without water under a scorching sun. Water spilled from the corners of her mouth, dribbling down her chin and mirroring the pathos of a suckling infant. Their child, though, would never imbibe life-giving nourishment from its mother's breast, and Gertrude would never experience the completeness of motherhood.

'Ivan unfurled his wife's fingers from the emptied mug and took it away. Gertrude picked up the child, drew it tight to her body and rocked gently to and fro, lowering her chin on the infant's head, whispering words that she hoped might resurrect life. But the infant was already growing cold.

CHAPTER 31

'Thunderstorms rumbled on through the night, throughout the next day, the next night and beyond and it seemed the storm would continue forever. The devil was at work, and Ivan believed that for as long as the infant remained unburied and in their home, their lives would continue to be blighted. He took a stick, wrapped fat-soaked rags around one end and pushed it into the fire, waiting until it ignited. Stinking black smoke filled the room, and Ivan hurried with it towards the door, almost tearing the door from its hinges in his eagerness to open it. He stepped out into the heavy rain, a lip twisted and his mouth fell open.

'"Lord, halt this foul rain," he roared, turning and watching, as Gertrude ambled into the doorway, carrying the bundled-up infant in her arms. On her head she wore a hood, fashioned from a scarf that hid her face, supporting the impression that only a ghostly void resided within. She looked up to the heavens and closed her eyes; her lips moved as if in silent prayer. "What use are your prayers?" Mocked Ivan, taking a spade and tramping on through the mud. The flaming torch hissed and spat, but the rain could not quell the flame. Above him, blue and orange light collided in the sky, fuelling the thunder. A thunderbolt stuck the ground at his feet, sending him reeling in the mud. "Damn this storm… This filth," he raged, sitting on the sodden earth, fighting away the grassy clods that rained upon him. "Damn this vileness, this Godforsaken foul life." He spat, jumped to his feet, shaking a fist at the heavens. "Damn all!" He turned to his wife. "Hurry, damn you. We haven't got all night."

'Gertrude opened her eyes and glanced briefly to him, before re-closing them, angling her head heavenwards and allowing the rain to wash over her, cleanse the stain left behind from her tears.

'"Hurry, wretch!" Hollered Ivan. "This storm will not stop while that thing remains…" He curtailed is anger and turned from her, mumbling.

'"This is not right, Murdac," protested Gertrude, reopening her eyes.

'"Right! Who has the right to say it is not? Who will know? Who will care? Better get that thing under the sod before –"

'"*Thing*!" Interrupted Gertrude, 'it is our child –"

'"Flesh and blood of the devil."

'"Then the child inherits its evil from you!"

'"Shut the door and hurry wretch," Ivan bid her, halting and watching her slam the door, waiting for her to catch up. They walked on together in silence. Lightning lit up the dismal night; thunder boomed a split second later and it became impossible to know which crash belonged to which strike. Gertrude, mumbling, pleaded with the Lord to be granted respite from the storm, to be allowed to lay the body of their child in the earth in peace.

'"Stop your blubbing and hurry."

'"You are a cruel, vile man, Murdac. Have you no mercy?"

'Ivan ignored her and pressed on. The wind gusted hard, whipping the rotting vegetation from the forest floor, flinging the vileness in their faces. Ivan spat the foulness from his lips, like a child after being administered bitter medicine. He halted abruptly, and Gertrude, following close behind him with her head down, slammed into his back.

'"Halt, witch! Halt, damn you!" He yelled, raising the

spade. Gertrude cowered and shielded her face with a hand.

'"How much further must we tread, Murdac?" She demanded, peering at him through splayed fingers. Ivan returned a scornful glance and forged ahead. "Murdac!" Gertrude screamed, removing her hand from her face.

'"The further from the cottage we step, the further that loathsome thing takes its evil."

'"Cruel, despicable beast! You know the distance will be too great for me to walk to tend our child's grave."

'Ivan waited for his wife to catch up: "You'll see the grave of that thing no more. Now, silence your tongue, or I swear I'll, I'll…" A vicious squall arrested his vitriol and the rain extinguished the flame. "Damn this rain, damn all!" He roared, hurling the torch to the ground, turning frantically in every direction. It was pitch black and in the darkness his wife was lost to him. "Gertrude, where are you, wife?" He appealed, groping blindly, but Gertrude remained silent and still. "Speak, dear wife. Come to me my love. Rescue me from this terrible blackness."

'Separated from his wife, his nursemaid, his mother, his slave, Ivan revealed his true character. No more the cowardly brute, inflicting suffering on lesser mortals, or cajoling the weak-willed into ill-advised deeds. Alone in the darkness, he epitomised a lost soul, his plea mirroring the cry of an infant on becoming detached from its mother's nipple. The lightning exposed Gertrude's silhouette and Ivan raced towards her, but the darkness, as if taunting, beat him.

'"Wife, where are you, wife? Wife…!" He called out with increasing irritation, and when she did not reply, his rage resurfaced. "Speak, wretch, speak damn it or I'll, I'll…" He halted and listened in the hope that he might hear her breathing, and then in the lightning he saw her.

She was close by; he reached out, grabbed hold of her and drew her into his powerful arms. "Don't think to flee from me again," he warned, dragging her along.

'"Let me alone, brute," she protested, digging her heels into the earth. The earth, though, was soft; Gertrude was weak and she knew resistance was futile. Ivan halted suddenly, inclined his head and listened.

'"No-o! Please God no!" He pleaded, letting go of Gertrude, clamping his hands to his ears. "No-o-o-o."

'"What is it? What is it you hear, Murdac?"

'"The wind," laughed Ivan, nervously. 'The wind's trickery, its treachery."

'But there was no wind. Gertrude seized her chance and backed stealthily away; she was about to turn and flee, but Ivan saw her.

'"Wait where you are, witch!" He hollered, raising the spade. "Or by God I'll gouge you apart and throw your entrails for the jackdaws."

'"If the lightning should strike you dead, Murdac, I should dance on your heart, piss on your face and cheer, spiteful beast!"

'Ivan stared at her, sneering, before setting about his task, digging a grave in the soft earth. Gertrude watched him, smiling when his spade struck a stone or snagged on a tree root, more so when the strain of his task caused a blood vessel in his nose to rupture. Blood spilled over his lips, he tasted blood – his blood, and he spat as if he had tasted poison, threw his head back and howled like a wolf.

'The storm quietened, the rain ceased to fall and hardly a breath of wind could be felt. But *that* noise, *that* incessant howling, Ivan was tormented by it. Anguished and yelling, he hurled the spade to the ground and pummelled his head with his fists. "Lord!" He cried out, looking to the sky. "For God's sake end this torture." Wild-eyed, he faced

Gertrude. "'Tis the work of the devil." He said, pointing to the child in her arms. "That devil will see us to our graves!"

'Lighting slammed into the earth and Ivan was thrown onto his back into the grave he had dug, and mother and child were separated.

'"My baby, my baby!" Screamed Gertrude, scrambling after her child. Its body convulsed in the lightning, exciting her momentarily, giving cause to believe that a miracle had been granted and life had been restored. But the child's body glowed brighter and brighter, the air turned putrid and when the fire had died all that remained of the child was a blackened skeleton. "Cruel God, thou hast deceived," ranted Gertrude.

'Fire raged about them, it threatened the existence of every living creature. But for Ivan and Gertrude, the threat to their lives would arise from a different source.

'"Voices!" Gertrude said suddenly, rising to her feet, angling her head, listening in order to determine if the voices she heard were real, or the machinations of a distempered brain.

'"Voices…?" Ivan questioned, dismissive of her and picking up the spade, using the blade to scrape the blackened remains into the pit he had dug.

'"Murdac, no!" Pleaded Gertrude, rushing at Ivan and striking him with clenched fists, again and again. He absorbed the blows unflinchingly and continued with his task, covering the skeleton with soil, hiding from sight all evidence of their ill-fated child. All the while, the voices in the forest grew louder. Gertrude reached out and grabbed hold of her husband's shirtsleeve. "Hear them, Murdac, voices!"

'"Get away from me!" Ivan raged, shaking her from him, pushing her violently away, but Gertrude flew back, clawing and mauling.

'"People from the village, they come for us –"

'"No one comes... Get away from me, hag." He struck her with a backward blow that sent her reeling in the mud. Gertrude remained on the earth where she fell and watched until Ivan had completed his work. When no trace of their child was left, Ivan slung the spade over a shoulder and hoisted Gertrude to her feet.

'"Let go of me brute," she screamed, breaking free. "I should have murdered you years ago as you slept, Murdac."

'Ivan sneered, but a smile broke upon his lips and he offered his hand. "Let's not fight, wife. Come, my love, we have suffered enough. Let's go home... Shelter from this foul night."

'Gertrude eyed him with suspicion, and as Ivan stepped nearer she matched his advancing stride with a backward step, but Ivan's hand found hers. She flinched, yet she discovered a touch so tender it would have been unrecognisable as the hand of her husband's had she not seen him in front of her with her own eyes. She surrendered. After all, to whom could she go? She had only Ivan. They were alone, two ostracised souls in the vastness of the world with no one but each other for guidance and comfort. Gertrude again flinched, not because she was afraid of her husband.

'"Voices, Ivan!" She said nervously, her eyes widening in anguish.

'"There are no voices, wife. It's your mind that torments you." 'Ivan attempted to convince her. His hands found her hips and he drew her closer, their lips touched and the Murdacs kissed; not with the passion of young lovers, but with sincerity ripened from the years of togetherness.

'"It's not my imagination. I am not mad and nor do I dream. Listen Ivan. Hear them; voices chanting."

'"Voices chanting?" Ivan repeated, staring distractedly into the depths of the forest. He inclined his head and listened, the thunder caused him to start. "Come, wife, we must hurry home before…" He halted mid-sentence, listening again, but still he could hear nothing.

'"We must not return to our home," urged Gertrude, taking hold of his arm, imploring a change of direction. His resistance caused her fingernails to sink into his flesh and Ivan's contempt exploded.

'"Wretched witch!" He yelled, shaking himself free, jabbing the spade into her body. "Get away from me."

'"Murdac! No!" She pleaded, her eyes widening with terror, as she watched him hoist the spade high above his head. Gertrude cowered and buried her head under her arms, bracing herself for the blow she felt certain would strike. The anticipated pain failed to arrive and when she next looked, she saw Ivan's silhouette, statuesque and still. The spade, having half-covered its course, halted mid-flight, its steel blade glinting in the lightning.

'"Look!" Implored Ivan, pointing with the spade in the direction of a shifting orange glow that projected its light above the treetops. The voices were loud, growing louder, and their words were worryingly clear.

'"Death to the devil and his witch," they chanted.

'Ivan and Gertrude knew that they must flee. But in which direction, and to where? They were hungry and cold, spent of strength with no energy to run and no courage to stand their ground and fight. It was like in a terrifying nightmare where leaden legs work fast and furious, but fail to advance an inch. The orange light glowed brighter; the chanting grew louder and angrier. Ivan and Gertrude were like hunted prey; wounded and unable to flee. In the confusion, wrought about by the storm, the pair were torn apart. Evil, this time, favoured the predators.

'The advancing army was bedraggled; they were soaked to the skin, footsore and muddied, bloodied and bruised and in pain. But their pain was an astringent, keeping them alert, lengthening their stride and driving them on. The village that they had left behind was deserted of all but the infirm. Every able-bodied person, young and old had, on that turbulent night, forsaken the comfort of their homes to march through the rain to Blackdaw Cottage, to effect vengeance for their dead children, to seek justice for sons and daughters, brothers and sisters whose lives had been snatched from them. Gabriel Mayhew was the man that led them.

'"Forward!" He roared, standing aside, slapping their backs as they passed, rousing them. He raced to the front to lead, urging them on with a wave. "Forward, friends," Gabriel repeated. "Soon we will be upon the house of evil."

'"To Blackdaw Cottage," the marchers yelled. '"Death to the devil and his witch."

'When the roof of Blackdaw Cottage came into view, Gabriel halted and turned: "A hundred yards more!" He called out, pausing when a cheer rang out. "One hundred yards more and we will be upon the door of evil. Be alert, all of you. The evil pair must not escape." His words were met with cheers; impassioned cheers of an avenging army.

'But when they reached the cottage they discovered it was empty. Feeling cheated, their anger erupted. They entered the building, ransacked the cottage and set it on fire, dancing and cheering as they witnessed its destruction; they left it ablaze and set out in search of the Murdacs.

'"Death to the devil and his witch," they chanted.

'Intelligent rational human beings, men, women and children, servants of God, had been transformed into an avenging mob. They had tasted the poison of hatred and were drunk on its toxin. The villagers that night would return to their homes with the stain of death upon their hands; yet not one person laid a finger on the doomed pair.

CHAPTER 32

'Ivan could hear the voices loud and clear, and his thoughts returned to happier times; to days when he and Gertrude were in love; idyllic days when their troubles could be dismissed with laughter and kisses. Those days were long gone, destroyed beyond redemption by a brutal act one desolate winter day. The weather was harsh and the pair starving, when Ivan, half-mad from hunger, his mind agitating in that diminished state, committed an act so deplorable Gertrude could never forgive. Skinned, a cat and a rabbit look much alike, and Ivan thought that she would not notice. He was too weak to go hunt for food that would sustain them, yet Ivan produced a fresh carcass dressed and ready for the pot. Gertrude, excited at the chance of tasting fresh meat, cooked the animal, but the instant she put the meat to her lips, she knew that it was not rabbit. Spitting and ranting, she jumped from her chair, screaming.

'"Rabbit, Murdac! This is not rabbit. This is the flesh of Snowflash." She raged, jabbing him repeatedly with the fork. "Selfish, brute, you'll one day live to regret your cruelty."

'Gertrude was right; evil committed begets only greater evil, and those words reverberated uncomfortably inside Ivan's head. For him it had proved a double travesty; Gertrude's beloved cat was dead, and she forbade him from consuming a morsel of its flesh. Yet they were starving slowly to death; without food to nourish their weakening bodies, they knew they could not survive much longer. Gertrude kicked Ivan out of their home one bitter day to find food, ordering him not to return empty-handed. Ivan searched fruitlessly for hours, growing wearier and more desperate with each passing minute, but he dare not return home without food. When he felt he could go no further, he noticed footprints in the snow – human footprints that he knew were not his. He followed the tracks and came upon the gamekeeper, crouched and aiming his gun at a pheasant. A shot was fired but the pheasant flew to safety, and while the gamekeeper was distracted, cursing his poor shot, reloading his gun, Ivan crept behind him armed with a sturdy branch he had pulled from beneath the snow…

'"Murdac!" Yelled Gertrude, startling Ivan and rousing him from his thoughts. "Over here."

'"Speak again, wife!" He implored. Lightning lit up the land, it echoed unnerving through the forest, sounding like the cackling of demented witches. Ivan saw Gertrude in the oscillating light and raced to her; they embraced like they had not done in years. "I thought I was never to see you again, wife. I thought you had taken your chance and fled. Left me forever."

'"Where could I go, and to whom? I have only you, Ivan."

'"The people want only me. You can yet escape, wife," he said, pushing her gently away. "Go, wife, save yourself."

'"Those fools blame us both for the ills that afflict their children. They blame us if they sneeze, they blame us for the rain, they blame us if they trip and fall over. They'll not be satisfied until we are both roasting in the fires of hell. They seek vengeance and will not rest until they have it. Hear them, Murdac! Angry people, people thirsty for blood; emotional people who believe only what they wish." Life had treated the Murdacs harshly and they welcomed the chance to begin anew. "I'll not leave you, Murdac. We've struggled together through life, and together we'll perish." Gertrude said, looking past him, gasping. "Our home, Ivan!" She blurted, witnessing flames leaping high into the night sky. "Our home is on fire and all that we possess burns with it."

'Ivan was calm. "Let it burn, wife. What use is any of it to us now?"

'Death's insatiable mouth widened. Lightning flashed and volley upon volley of thunder boomed, culminating in an explosion that split apart the sky. From the widening fissure, a light too painful to look upon descended earthwards, spewing an iridescent white mist that churned with dizzying speed, assuming the image of the avenging feline, carrying in its paw a triple-pronged spear. Ivan and Gertrude lifted their hands to shield their eyes, but the light could not be shut out; it glowed brighter and fiercer, burning deep into their souls, purging...'

There the storyteller faltered and halted. Squinting, he lifted a hand up to his eyes, as if the same dazzling light troubled him also.

'No, no...' Bentley, distractedly beseeched, before rousing himself, noticing the children's eyes upon him. Chuckling nervously, he forced a smile. His cheeks had turned white to match his beard, and he fought hard for every breath. Clutching his chest with one hand, he fumbled at his side with his other. Finding the glass tumbler and lifting it to his lips, gulping greedily the remainder of the whisky from it.

'Well, well children!' He chuckled, setting the tumbler back down on the floor. 'Right, where was I now? Ah... Yes...'

The tale resumed.

'The bright light in the sky... The descending mists...

Well, Ivan and Gertrude were doomed, they were trapped beneath the spotlight from heaven, like rabbits mesmerised in the glare of a motor car's headlights, unable to move and awaiting their fate.

'"There they are!" A voice called out. Eyes all turned upon the pair and fingers were pointed. "Death to the devil and his witch," the mob yelled, surging closer, hurling blazing torches, picking up sticks and stones from the mud and throwing them at the terrified pair, chanting. But when the mob was about to move in and seize their quarry, lightning rammed into the earth between them and prevented them from progressing further, and there, the oscillating beam remained, acting as a shield, repelling all missiles. The light intensified until it became too painful to look upon, and afterwards, when light and the mists had cleared, the spot where Ivan and Gertrude Murdac had stood was empty.

'Gabriel Mayhew and his army looked on, dumbfounded. Feeling cheated, some angled their heads heavenwards, raised clenched fists and cursed the Lord for betraying them. A thunderbolt thudded into the earth and silenced their blaspheming.

'"Friends!" Gabriel called out. "No more harsh words – give thanks to the Lord, and be proud of what we have tonight achieved. Our duty to our children is done. The Lord has raised the storm to affect justice; his kind deed has steered us from committing evil of our own; for that we must all be thankful. Go home, friends. Our mission has been accomplished: there is no more to be done. Return to your homes, good people and celebrate. The plague is finished and will no more strike our children. Go home."

'Whether by God's hand, good fortune, coincidence, or the determined will of the people, no more children were infected by the plague, and no more died. The suffering that the villagers had endured for many months ended with the demise of Ivan and Gertrude Murdac.'

And there Bentley's story ended.

CHAPTER 33

The instant that the final word of the final sentence of the final chapter slipped from Bentley's lips, he slumped in his chair, exhausted. His breathing turned irregular and laboured and he fought hard to keep those misted eyes open. Yet despite his discomfort he smiled; his smile, though, was one of relief for, after the years carrying with him the parable of Ivan and Gertrude Murdac, he was at last free of its encumbrance. The story, imprinted upon the minds of the three children, would not now be lost with his demise. The old man's eyes remained with the children, but his smile began to fade, his gaze grew distant and it was as if he saw nothing of the present and looked out upon some future destination. He roused himself one final time:

'Children... It's, it's terribly late,' he mouthed. 'Bed, bedtime... Look out for each other... I'm done for, I'm, I'm...' Tired eyelids closed over those emerald eyes, and tremulous lips slipped apart. Bentley, it appeared, wished to speak, but could not and was lost to deserving sleep. The effort expended reciting the tale had proved too great and had drained all his strength. The children looked to their friend; they looked to each other, unsure what they should next do. Morton stood and stepped up to the sleeping man.

'Is he dead?' He wondered, scrutinising the old man's face.

'Course he's not dead,' said Abigail.

'He's fallen asleep, fast asleep,' decided Ruth.

Morton remained unconvinced and pushed his face to within inches of Bentley's. The old man twitched, his mouth fell open and a snore rattled in his throat. Morton lurched back, laughing nervously, backing slowly away, satisfied that life remained in Bentleys' worn out body.

Ruth, yawning and stretching, shivered; she too was tired, her body craved warmth and sleep. Sputnik, aware of his mistress's movements, rose from the hearth yawing and stretching also, looking to her. The cat shifted; she stood, sharpened her claws on the stone floor, while looking about. But seeing nothing of interest, she lay back down and curled up under the diminishing heat from the dying fire. Ruth took the small shovel from the hearth and used it to scoop the spent ash from beneath the grate, which she scattered over the embers. With luck the fire would remain alive until morning.

'I'm tired,' complained Abigail, yawning. 'And I'm cold.' She said, squinting at the face of her wristwatch. 'It's nearly half past eleven!' She exclaimed, sighing. 'Oh, if only I was at home in my nice warm bed!'

'Well, you're not,' said Morton, somewhat abruptly. 'And I'm glad I'm not.'

Ruth unhooked the lamp from the wire and, holding it chest-high, carried it to the window. She lifted the hessian curtain aside and used it to clear the condensation from a glass pane and attempted to look outside, but snow covered the entire window and nothing was visible.

'It's probably snowing still,' she remarked casually, letting go of the curtain and facing her friends. 'It must be ten feet deep by now.'

'Ten feet!' Morton's animation returned life to a tiring body.

Ruth's speculation, regarding the depth of the snow, was perhaps the first figure that had entered her head, but much snow had fallen that night and her guess was not as wildly overstated as might be imagined. Deep snowdrifts had formed everywhere under the wind, deep enough to engulf entire cottages. Abigail and Morton joined Ruth at the window. Morton pulled the curtain aside and looked at the snow-covered windows.

'Wow! It'll be weeks before we can go home.'

'Weeks!' Abigail recoiled at the thought. 'But we'll freeze to death, or starve if we have to stay here for weeks,' she said gloomily, stepping from the window, hunching her shoulders and shivering.

'We won't starve,' Morton reassured her. 'There's tons of food. You've seen it! And loads of firewood in the shed… Anyway I'm never going home, not ever.'

'Dad and Jack'll come and rescue us tomorrow, you'll see,' Ruth said confidently.

'But how will they know we are here?' Abigail asked.

Ruth shrugged. 'They just will.'

'I hope they don't ever come and rescue us,' said Morton.

'Well, I do,' Abigail responded, yawning. 'I want to go to sleep, but not in Bentley's bed.'

'It'll be all right,' Ruth assured her, setting off towards the door that led into the bedroom, 'and it'll only be for one night.' Sputnik raced after her.

'Where's Bentley going to sleep?' Asked Morton.

'He's asleep already in his chair,' Abigail reminded him.

'And he'll have to stay there,' Ruth said, disappearing into the bedroom. 'There's no room for him in here.'

Abigail and Morton followed.

'It's cold,' said Abigail, as she entered the bedroom. 'And it's scary.'

'Sputnik'll keep guard while we're asleep, won't you, Sputnik?' Ruth said, bending and stroking her dog.

The children looked about the room; they looked to

each other, but then Elsa entered, meowing, and distracting them. The cat, after glancing briefly about, jumped up on the chair positioned close by the bed; she sniffed the cushion and clawed it, before settling into its hollow centre and curling up. It was where Elsa perhaps slept each night, watching over her master, ready to warn him of approaching intruders.

Ruth set the lamp down carefully on the upended orange box that sufficed as a bedside cabinet. Abigail folded back the covers on the bed; the square creases confirmed that the sheets had indeed been changed, as Bentley had claimed. She meandered round to the opposite side of the bed, joining Morton.

'Are you getting undressed?' He asked her.

'I am not,' Abigail responded firmly. 'And anyway I haven't got my pyjamas. Are you getting undressed?'

'Not likely. Not in front of girls.'

Ruth lowered herself onto the edge of the bed and removed her wellington boots. Abigail and Morton observing did likewise.

'Where are you sleeping?' Abigail asked Morton.

'There's only one bed,' Ruth reminded them.

'I'm not sleeping on the floor, if that's what you think,' Morton informed her.

'Mum won't like it if I sleep in bed with a boy.'

'Well, you can sleep on the floor, then, 'cause I'm not,' Morton responded. 'And anyway, your mum won't know if you don't tell her. I won't tell anybody.'

'Nor me,' agreed Ruth.

'But it's wrong to tell lies,' stressed Abigail.

'Well, not telling is not really telling a lie, is it?'

Abigail became thoughtful. She knew that, once reunited, her mother would probe her for every last detail of the night she spent at Blackdaw Cottage, and the truth would be teased from her, bit by bit.

'Mmm… I suppose I could not tell mum everything… Be economical with the truth.'

'Economical with the truth?' Queried Morton, frowning.

'Well… I don't right know what it means,' admitted Abigail, ' but dad says it's what politicians do when they tell lies – when they don't want to tell the truth, but when they don't want people to know they tell lies. So I guess it must mean it's all right to tell lies – well, sometimes anyway.'

'I tell lies to my dad all the time,' boasted Morton. 'If I didn't I'd get into lots more trouble.'

'I'm glad my dad's not like your dad,' Abigail said.

'Sometimes he's all right,' Morton began, unconvincingly. 'But…' He halted mid-sentence, straightening his socks after half-dragging them from his feet. The children stood on the cold floor in their stockinged feet, eyeing the bed with trepidation, looking to each other, each imploring the other to make the first move.

'You can sleep in the middle,' Ruth said suddenly, looking to Morton.

'I'm not sleeping between two girls,' he protested.

'Well, I'm not sleeping in the middle,' Abigail said.

'Nor me,' added Ruth.

'There, that's two against one,' declared Abigail. 'You're outvoted. You'll have to sleep in the middle whether you like to or not, Morton Rymer.'

'It's not fair.'

'Please, Morton!' Pleaded Ruth. 'It'll be warmest in the middle.'

'Why should I?'

Ruth continued her appeal with an imploring stare. Morton sighed; he was cold and too tired to argue and he knew that standing about on the freezing floor, disputing who should sleep where would produce only chilblains and solve nothing.

'Oh, all right then,' Morton conceded grudgingly. Without further hesitation he threw back the sheets, leaped onto the uninviting bed and shuffled to the centre where he lay on his back with his arms folded across his chest. The two girls looked to him and their glances met across the bed under the flickering lamplight. They giggled.

'Hurry up, will you!' Morton implored. 'It's freezing.'

'Which side do you want to sleep, Ruth?' Asked Abigail.

'Any. I'm not bothered,' replied Ruth, shrugging. 'You say.'

'I'm not bothered either. You say.'

'Hurry, will you, before I freeze to death,' urged Morton.

Abigail climbed onto the bed at the side where she stood, shuffled up to Morton and lay alongside him, tugging the sheets up to her neck, smiling and facing him.

'About time too,' he said.

'Here, Sputnik!' Ruth called to her dog, patting the sheet she had spread out on the floor at the side of the bed. Sputnik stepped on to it, looking to her and wagging his tail. 'Lie down.' The dog sniffed the sheet before lying down on it. 'Good boy.'

Once Sputnik was settled, Ruth looked to her friends on the bed and threw back the sheets. She snuffed out the lamp, plunging the room into darkness, and jumped up on the bed, shuffling quickly into position and pulling the covers up over her.

Inhibition gave way to instinct, and the three children slipped from sight beneath the covers and snuggled together for the night. There on that cold bleak night in the forest, protected within the crumbling walls of Blackdaw Cottage, the three children succumbed swiftly to deep slumber.

It was late, about midnight, when the snow finally stopped falling, but the wind continued its mischief, piling the cold crystals into ever deepening drifts. Stars sparkled under the naked night sky and the moon, watching over earth from its lofty elevation, standing guard over the inhabitants of the cold cottage, seemed to shiver also. That night, the temperature across all England plummeted like a stone, falling to – 14 degrees centigrade. Jack Frost's fingers indeed probed deep, as he distributed his icy hoar to homes across the entire land, more so in houses where the fires burned low or not at all, snuffing out the lives of many an unwary sleeper, while they were at their most vulnerable, as they slept.

CHAPTER 34

Mrs Evison rose early the next morning after a sleepless night, setting about the tasks awaiting her attention. The cooker was first on a mental list of many, needing raking and re-fuelling. She removed the metal plug from the hob with a small poker and then stoked the coals. At the bottom of the dark hole she glimpsed a glimmer of red and smiled. After putting the poker aside, she lifted the scuttle up from the floor and emptied in coal. She replaced the plug, rinsed her hands in a basin of cold water; filled the kettle and a large pan with water from a milk churn, placing them on separate hobs. Then, from a cardboard packet, she shook a measure of oats into the pan of warming water, stirring gently. Plates and dishes left overnight on the draining board to dry were put away. Bacon was carried from the pantry, the foil covering removed and slices carved from the joint. The slices were arranged into two rows in two large trays; a third tray was filled with sausages. The porridge was again stirred, and milk was poured into the pan of thickening oats.

Like Mrs Evison, Mrs Markson had suffered a fraught and sleepless night, tossing and turning throughout. After hearing noises in the kitchen below she rose, dressing quickly in the cold bedroom and exiting, leaving her restless husband, buried from sight beneath the covers, sleeping.

The kettle boiled and the porridge bubbled. Mrs Evison slid the kettle from the hob, stirred the porridge and removed the pan from the heat. She spooned tea into a teapot, poured boiling water in from the kettle, leaving the tea to infuse before pouring a mug and relaxing in the chair by the cooker. She sipped slowly, savouring the flavour of the first brew of the morning.

Mrs Markson entered the kitchen, hunched and shivering.

'A cup of tea, Mrs Markson?' Mrs Evison asked, rising from her chair, sighing. She was mildly annoyed at being disturbed so soon after sitting down, but smiled.

'Oh, yes please,' Mrs Markson returned a warm smile.

'Come… Sit by the cooker where it's warm.'

'Thank you. I, I couldn't sleep… Thought I might as well get up and see if I could be of any use.'

'Well… A nice cup of tea first,' Mrs Evison said, gesticulating, directing her guest to the chair she had vacated. After sitting and receiving a mug of reviving tea, Mrs Markson glanced at the large pan on the hob and guessed it would be porridge; she smiled, wondering whose appetites might be receptive to food when their children remained lost in the blizzard. Her eyes met Mrs Evison's gaze.

'Any news of the children?'

'Nothing,' Mrs Evison replied, nipping her lips together. 'But we weren't expecting any just yet. Hopefully we'll know something before the day is over.'

'Good news, let's hope,' Mrs Markson dared hope, but her gloomy expression suggested that she did not anticipate good news.

'The children will be fine, I'm sure,' Mrs Evison said, attempting to reassure her.

'I wish I could be as confident. Another keen frost followed all that snow. And what of that strange man, Bentley?'

'Bentley's harmless – he won't harm children,' Mrs Evison assured her.

'If they've made it to that man's home,' Mrs Markson

said. 'Perhaps they didn't reach the cottage and have frozen to death in the snow, like Morton's father!'

'No, no, I'm sure…' Noises outside distracted Mrs Evison; she saw snow flying through the air and smiled. Jack had risen at the same time as she and was busy digging a path through the thigh-high snow to the tractor shed.

Jack reached the shed and opened the doors, looking immediately to the oil lamp set on the floor beneath the tractor. He smiled; its blue flame flickered still within the glass dome. He had last night lit the lamp and positioned it on the floor beneath the tractor's engine, hoping that the flame would provide sufficient warmth to keep the frost at bay and prevent the diesel from freezing up. He flicked on the light switch, lifted the lamp from the floor and snuffed out the flame. After setting the lamp aside, he climbed up onto the tractor, lowering himself gingerly onto the cold seat. Attached to the front of the tractor on two long metal arms, was fixed a large metal bucket. The implement was used for a variety of tasks about the farm. Today, providing the engine fired up successfully, it would be used to dig a path through the snow to Blackdaw Cottage.

Using a forefinger and thumb, Jack gripped the black knob situated knee-high on the dashboard and pulled it out. Holding it extended until white smoke flowed from a circular aluminium grill the size of a shilling, set higher on the dashboard. When the white smoke thickened, Jack released the knob and pressed the starter lever. The engine groaned lazily as the pistons turned agonisingly slowly. Grimacing, Jack released the lever and pulled the knob out once again. Waiting this time until the white smoke flowed liberally, this time keeping the knob extended while he pressed the starter lever. The engine again groaned slowly; it stuttered and spluttered and the pistons rattled, but this time black smoke leaped out from the exhaust funnel in agitated bursts and the engine sprung suddenly to life. Choking black smoke rebounded from the roof and enshrouded Jack, making him cough. The black smoke turned grey, the grey smoke turned white; it lightened and became invisible. After checking that the handbrake was securely engaged, Jack dismounted from the tractor and hurried into the doorway where he stood, filling his lungs with the cold, clean air.

Chatter and the sound of feet, scrunching through the snow, encouraged Jack to look round the corner of the shed. Jet bounded awkwardly over the snow towards him; the dog saw Jack and barked. The gamekeeper and blacksmith followed close behind, both were attired appropriately in heavy clothing worn beneath oilskin coats. Oilskin leggings were pulled down over wellington uppers to prevent the snow from falling inside, and both wore matching leather hats.

'Hard at work already!' Remarked Vargis, joining Jack in the doorway. 'Tractor started and running… Good man.'

Jack took several steps into the shed; Jet followed him, shaking snow from his coat. Vargis and Mr Gregory, reaching the cleared concrete, stamped their feet to dislodge the snow from their boots, before joining Jack inside the shed. The men stood surveying the snowy panorama, marvelling how in less than twelve hours everything had surrendered so absolutely to the snow. Save for the channel that Jack had dug out, snow lay smooth and deep smooth for as far as the eye could see. Fences and walls had all disappeared from sight, and the trees were skeletal white images protruding from an ocean of white. After indulging for only a few minutes, Jack led the men into the farmhouse, into the kitchen.

Mrs Evison smiled. 'Come on in, Mr Gregory, Mr Vargis.'

Mr Evison and Mr Markson were already seated at the table, spooning porridge into their mouths. Mrs Markson, sitting with them, scrutinised the rugged-looking men and acknowledged them with a nervous smile. She returned her attention to the porridge on the table in front of her, having no appetite, she chased dark flecks about the bowl with her spoon.

'Come, come and sit where it's warm,' Mrs Evison said.

'I'm fine here, thank you,' said Vargis, repositioning a chair set near to the entrance, sitting. He unfastened the buckle under his chin and pulled off his hat, issuing orders to his dog to sit on the mat at his feet. 'Better not get too comfortable.'

The blacksmith pulled up a second chair; he set it down alongside the gamekeeper and sat. Jack, after rinsing his hands in the sink, drying them on a towel, took his seat at the table next to his dad. His mother placed a bowl of steaming porridge in front of him; and the hungry young man, after stirring two spoonfuls of amber-coloured syrup into the bowl of porridge, added milk and ate hurriedly.

'You'll have some breakfast, won't you?' Mrs Evison asked, looking to the gamekeeper and blacksmith.

'Well, I... I had a little before leaving home,' stuttered Vargis.

'Of course they'll have some breakfast,' Mr Evison intervened. 'We might be out all day in the cold.'

'Porridge?'

'A bacon sandwich will do me, Mrs Evison, thank you,' the blacksmith said.

'The same for me, if it's no trouble,' the gamekeeper returned, smiling.

'Bacon sandwiches for two,' Mrs Evison said.

She cracked eggs into a tray of hot fat until there was

no room for any more, opened the oven door and pushed the tray inside. No sooner had she closed the oven door, her husband released the spoon noisily into his dish, signalling to her that he was ready for the next course.

'Eggs won't be long,' Ms Evison said. She poured tea into two mugs and carried them to Vargis and Mr Gregory. Returning, she removed the trays of crisped bacon from the oven and made sandwiches, arranging them onto two plates and carrying the sandwiches to the men waiting by the entrance. Jet rose and looked expectantly to her, licking his salivating jowls.

'Down, hound!' Snapped Vargis. 'Sit!' Jet obeyed immediately and sat on his hindquarters, watching as his master bit into a sandwich. 'Mmm… Delicious, Thank you, Mrs Evison – too good for you, mutt.'

The blacksmith picked up a sandwich and ate with relish too, and Mrs Evison, after retreating, returned hurriedly with bacon scraps concealed in a hand.

'Your dog will eat these, won't he, Mr Vargis?' She asked, unfurling her fingers.

Vargis, chewing, nodded. 'He'll eat anything you care to give him.'

'Terrible what happened to Mr Rymer, wasn't it?' Mrs Evison said, wiping her hands on her pinny after throwing the scraps on the mat for the dog. 'Poor Morton.'

Both men stopped chewing and looked to Mrs Evison.

'Eh! What! What's happened to Rymer?' Asked Vargis, chewing, slowly.

'Haven't you heard! He was found dead at the wheel of his car last night.'

'Rymer, dead…!' Mr Gregory said.

'His car skidded on the ice, hit a wall and overturned.'

Vargis gulped down several mouthfuls of tea and cleared his throat. 'Rymer wasn't much liked, but it's sad when a life ends all the same. And it'll be a sorry time for Morton.' He set his mug down on the floor and bit into the sandwich.

'The police found his car in a snow-filled ditch, Mr Rymer was trapped inside. Poor man froze to death.' Mrs Evison said, before turning and walking away.

The two men's jaws quickened. Thoughts returned to the living or to those they hoped lived still. Mrs Markson released the spoon into the bowl of porridge and pushed it away.

'I'm sorry, Mrs Evison, but I can't –'

'Don't worry, the dogs'll enjoy it,' Mrs Evison said, forcing a smile.

Mrs Markson turned to her husband: 'Don't now what I, we'd do, Clive, if –'

'The children will be fine,' Mrs Evison stressed. 'Having the time of their lives. Ruth will, if I know her.'

Mrs Markson sniffed; she dabbed the corners of her eyes with a handkerchief she removed from the sleeve of her jumper. Mr Markson placed an arm around his wife's shoulders and drew her gently to him.

'Everything will turn out fine, I'm sure,' he said.

Mrs Markson forced a smile. Mr Markson smiled; his smile widening when Mrs Evison set plates of eggs, bacon, sausages, tomatoes and fried bread on the table in front of the three men.

'I'll prepare some flasks of coffee for you to take with you,' Mrs Evison said. 'Hot, sweet, milky coffee. Ruth likes it that way.'

'They'll be hungry also, I expect!' Mr Evison said, cutting a rasher of bacon in two and forking half into his mouth.

'Yes, yes… I'm preparing bacon sandwiches for them, and there's a box of chocolate fingers in the pantry; Ruth's favourite. Morton also likes them.'

'Abigail will eat anything covered in chocolate,' smiled Mrs Markson, pushing the handkerchief back up the sleeve of her jumper. She stood: 'Can I do anything to help, Mrs Evison?' She asked, stepping to the sink and rinsing her hands in the bowl of water.

'Thank you… You can finish making the sandwiches. More sandwiches, Mr Vargis, Mr Gregory?'

Both men declined, mindful of the urgency of the task awaiting them, knowing that the journey to Blackdaw Cottage would be long, arduous and dangerous. They all prayed that the gamekeeper would be proved right, and that the children would be found safe and well at the cottage. All were aware that no human, exposed to the hostile night, could have survived without shelter. But if the children had found their way through the snow to the cottage, there could be no guarantee they had had survived the arctic night.

CHAPTER 35

Jack was the last to begin breakfast but he was the first to finish. He picked up the scarf that had been warming on the handle of the cooker and wrapped it around his neck, took the sleeveless jerkin from the back of a chair and put it on. He threaded his arms through the heavy black overcoat his mother held open for him, helping him on with it over the bulky leather jerkin.

'That's me ready,' said Jack, pulling a balaclava on over his head.

'Will you be warm enough, Jack?' Asked his mother, adjusting his collar and straightening his scarf. 'You'll be sat motionless on that cold tractor seat for hours.'

'Stop fussing, mum. An Eskimo would sweat wearing this lot,' he protested, turning. 'I'll get the trailer hitched, dad… Grab some shovels while you finish breakfast.

'Aye, all right, Jack. We'll not be long.'

'Need any help to get the trailer hitched?' Asked Mr Gregory.

'No, no, I can manage, thank you,' Jack said, stepping towards the door, taking hold of the handle. 'Ten minutes.'

'Be careful, won't you, Jack?' urged his mother, turning and looking towards the door, but Jack had already exited the kitchen. The door closed and she stood staring at it, before facing her husband. 'You'll keep an eye on him, won't you? And take one of Jack's balaclavas for yourself. It'll keep your ears warm. I don't want to listen to you complaining about earache for the remainder of the winter.' She hastened from the kitchen, unaware of her husband's disapproving frown.

Vargis held up his hat. 'Kids might make fun, but it keeps my ears warm.'

'It's not only the kids who make fun of you,' mocked the blacksmith. Vargis turned and glared, before smiling wryly.

'This'll keep you nice and warm,' said Mrs Evison, returning with a red balaclava and handing it to her husband. His frown returned, but he pulled the hat over his head.

'You'll not get lost in that,' laughed the blacksmith. 'You look like a live match.'

'Don't listen to him,' Mrs Evison said, smiling affectionately, as she straightened the balaclava, bent and kissed her husband's cheek.

'No time for that,' he said irritably, brushing her gently aside and standing. 'Come on, let's get going. Jack'll be waiting… Spare coats in the hall.' He said, motioning to Vargis and Mr Gregory. 'And a warm hat!' He added, turning to Mr Markson.

'I've got a very good hood on my duffel coat,' Mr Markson said.

'You'll need something more robust than a duffel coat with a hood,' scoffed Mr Evison. He faced his wife. 'Find him a something to fit over his duffel coat… Warm scarves and coats for the children.'

Mrs Evison disappeared into the hall; she returned shortly with a coat for Mr Markson, hats, scarves and coats for the children, which she stuffed into a large plastic bag.

Jack coupled the trailer onto the towbar of the tractor – a trailer with chest-high sides and an open back. He loaded on shovels and spades of varying sizes, and when Jack drove the unit from the shed the men were all waiting in the porch, all suitably attired. Mrs Evison and Mrs Markson followed them outside, carrying bags stuffed with flasks of coffee and food.

Vargis climbed onto the trailer and whistled. His dog, Jet leapt eagerly on up, skidding on the slippery wooden floorboards. 'Steady, damn it, steady!'

The bags were passed up to the gamekeeper and arranged on the floor at the front of the trailer. The men all climbed on board.

'Have we got everything?' Asked Jack.

Mr Evison nodded: 'Aye, Jack, let's get going.'

'Be careful, won't you!' Mrs Evison called to her husband. 'And don't dare return without the children.'

'Keep moving, Clive,' Mrs Markson bid him. 'And do be careful.'

The two women watched as the tractor powered its way through the drifts of deep snow, they stood in the cold until the tractor and trailer had disappeared from sight.

'Come on, Lindsey.' Mrs Evison said, shivering. 'Let's get inside.'

The ladies hastened into the warm farmhouse, closing the door behind them. The rescue party was at last on underway, and they could only hope and pray that the mission would prove to be successful. But several fraught hours would pass before they could know that.

CHAPTER 36

It had turned seven o'clock on that bitter morning. The sky was flecked with stars of variable sizes and brightness, the moon was full and majestic; its sombre light lingering upon the surface of the snow, lightening their way, rendering the cold morning brighter than many an overcast winter day.

Jack steered the unit onto the farm driveway and the wind met them with all its hostile force, snow was lifted up from the ground and driven upon them; the icy crystals stung the men's cheeks, lips and noses. The enormous herringbone-patterned rear tyres struggled to find grip in the deep snow; the wheels spinning uselessly round and around, compacting the snow and turning it to ice; at times the tractor was able to move forward only slowly in a frustratingly, stuttering motion.

Tractor and trailer came to a complete standstill. Vargis and Mr Gregory jumped down from the trailer and began shovelling the snow away from around the tractor's wheels. When the wheels were able to secure grip, Jack lowered the bucket and charged into the snowdrift, lifting out bucketfuls of snow and dumping them aside, clearing a track that the tractor could pass through.

They reached the main road but progress was no swifter. Snow was blown upon them from over the walls and hedges, filling the road level with the top of the limestone walls. Snowdrift after snowdrift was cleared or ploughed through, snow was dug away from around a gate, the gate was opened and Jack drove the unit into the field. The field led to a larger field – the same field where the children had yesterday sledged down the steep hill before, for whatever reason, abandoning the sledge and walking into the forest.

In places where the snow lay shallow over the land, Vargis and Mr Gregory climbed back onto the trailer. And for a while, progress was relatively easy, until the tractor sunk up to its axle in a snow-filled hollow. After reversing, nudging forwards again and again, Jack did his utmost to drive the tractor free, but the rear wheels spun round and round and the unit was unable to move an inch, forwards or backwards. All hands were needed; a man to each wheel and, working hard and fast, the men cleared much of the snow away from the wheels. Jack was able to steer the tractor free, but time had been lost; over an hour had passed since they set out, and a considerable distance and considerable challenges lay ahead of them yet.

The stars had all melted into the brightening morning sky, but the ghostly image of the moon remained to watch over them, disappearing only when the sun revealed its fiery fullness over the horizon. Its slanting rays dazzled upon the snow, but its fire was impotent against the annoying north-easterly winds.

Jack zigzagged a precarious route up the hill until, but at the steepest point, momentum was lost and the wheels began to spin. The tractor could move forwards no further and began sliding backwards down the hill, slewing sideways and coming to a halt at a precarious angle on the hillside. Both tractor and trailer were in danger of jack-knifing and turning over. Jack ordered the men to dismount, and then began the delicate task of manoeuvring back and forth. Bit by bit the tractor and trailer was straightened and Jack was able to drive to the top of the hill.

Precious time had again been lost, and over two and a half hours had passed before they reached the perimeter of the forest. If anyone thought that the going would be easier, they were mistaken. In areas where the pine trees were planted thinly, the snow was exposed to the wind and driven into insurmountable drifts. Added to that, branches burdened under the accumulation of snow had broken from the trees, further littering their path.

'This is hopeless, Jack,' Mr Evison said, despondent and shaking his head. 'It'll be midnight before we reach the cottage at this rate.'

'We'll be lucky to reach the cottage at all,' ejaculated a distressed Mr Markson.

'We'll get there,' said Jack. 'Don't you worry. We must.'

Onwards they progressed, slowly and painfully. After one obstacle had been overcome another appeared, blocking their path and creating further work. A clearing was reached and the deep lying snow brought the tractor to a standstill yet again. Jack, the most optimistic, looked ahead at the obstacles blocking their way, and sighed deeply.

'Let's have tot of whisky,' suggested Mr Evison.

'Aye, a splendid idea,' agreed Vargis, rubbing his hands and smiling, finding the flask in the bag and passing it to Mr Evison. Mr Evison unscrewed the cap and swigged a draught of whisky, offering it next to Mr Markson. He, after wiping the bottleneck, sipped only the smallest of draughts and, coughing, thrust the flask in front of Hector Vargis.

The gamekeeper laughed. 'City folk, huh… No stomach for strong liquor.' He mocked, lifting the flask to his lips and swallowing a copious draft, demonstrating to Mr Markson how whisky should be taken. 'Dare say you'll get used to it given time – will if you remain in these cold parts.' He burped, drew a sleeve across his mouth, upended the flask once again and swigged some more.

'Leave some for me!' The blacksmith implored, snatching the flask from Vargis the instant it left his lips. After drinking some whisky, Mr Gregory offered the flask to Jack, but he declined and it was returned to Mr Evison who, after taking a further nip, replaced the cap and returned the whisky to the bag. Revitalised, the men got down to their task, toiling with renewed urgency until a path through the snowdrift had been cleared. The men climbed back onto the trailer and onward they progressed. Through narrow areas where the tractor could barely squeeze between the densely planted pines, trees whose snow-laden crowns hung low, brushing their heads and depositing a shower of snow over them.

Despondency at last gave rise to hope; the pine trees thinned out and wider shafts of sunlight penetrated the dark forest. In the distance through the snowy mist a chimney appeared, poking its presence above the snow-laden roof of a cottage, Blackdaw Cottage.

Jack checked his wristwatch; it had turned twelve o'clock. Five hours had passed since they set out that morning – five long hours of toil in the sub-zero temperatures. For five long hours the men had been tested physically and mentally, their strength never once wavering. Jack steered the tractor as close to the cottage as the snowdrift embracing the building would allow, he engaged the handbrake and, leaving the engine idling, dismounted. All was still and silent except for the caw of a jackdaw, the wind's incessant howl and the clatter of the tractor's pistons. Snowdrifts reached up to the eaves of the single-storied building, almost burying it from sight but, worryingly, snow lay smooth and undisturbed upon the ground, save for a spattering of animal's tiny footprints: proof that life existed in the icy isolation. Jack waded through the knee-deep snow towards the cottage, calling out his sister's name, but there came no answer. He paused before calling again; but again, no reply was forthcoming, and nor was there any reassuring bark from Sputnik.

Inside the cold cottage, Sputnik sat shivering on his hindquarters on his makeshift bed, alert to sounds that he could not quite make out, angling his head one way and then the other. The dog looked anxiously to the bed, whimpering, but he provoked no response from the children and the covers did not stir. Dispirited, Sputnik lay back down upon the cold sheet and curled up, keeping a restless eye upon the bed still.

Bentley's cat, Elsa had, at some point during the night jumped up on the bed and lay in a hollow. She, like Sputnik, remained uneasy, watchful and alert, uncertain whether the sounds should be welcomed, or feared. Yawning, the cat rose, arched her back and stretched, before jumping onto the floor close to Sputnik. The dog's eyelids flicked open and his eyeballs rotated as he traced the path of the restless cat. Elsa jumped back up onto the bed, meowing to rouse the dead, clawing at the bedspread, but the three children remained buried beneath the covers, silent and motionless.

Vargis jumped down from the trailer, pushing a wad of tobacco into his mouth – the first of the morning. Chewing slowly, he picked up two shovels from the trailer and carried them to where Jack stood, handing him one. The pair inched closer to the cottage.

'Odd!' He remarked, loosening the buckle under his chin, relieving his neck and stretching it, glancing up. 'No smoke rising from the chimney!' Jet, sauntering behind, remained uncharacteristically quiet. 'Bentley!'

The gamekeeper shouted, waiting several seconds before calling again. Hearing no reply, the two men set to work, digging a path through the waist-deep snow towards the cottage door. The blacksmith joined them, and soon the door to the cottage was reached. Vargis freed the frozen latch and then charged the door with a shoulder, but the door was bonded with snow and ice and refused to budge.

'Ruth!' Mr Evison called out, bustling his way to the door, thumping hard on it with a clenched fist. 'Ruth! Morton! Anybody!' He yelled, angling his head and listening.

'I don't like it,' said Mr Markson, joining them. 'I don't like it at all.'

'Can't understand why Sputnik hasn't barked,' said Jack.

'Stand back!' Mr Gregory called out, rushing forward and charging the door repeatedly with a shoulder until it gave way. After stumbling inside, the burly blacksmith was greeted by squadron of squawking jackdaws, flapping their wings agitatedly in the faces of the men, cawing. Vargis, following the blacksmith into the cottage with Jack, wafting the birds away a hand. Jet dashed between the men's legs and disappeared inside the dark room. Mr Markson and Mr Evison, entering, halted being startled by frenzied barking. Vargis, surveying the cold room in search of his dog, gasped out aloud upon seeing the hand of a man dangling over a chair arm by the dead fire. Jet nuzzled the wizened white fingers. Breathing heavy and chewing fast, the gamekeeper stepped up to the slumped figure in the chair.

'Bentley!' Vargis gently called, gripping the shoulder of the motionless man. Turning, he saw Mr Evison behind him, tugging off a glove, he slipped two fingers between the man's neck and scarf and turned to the gamekeeper, shaking his head:

'Poor man, he's like ice.'

What hope now for the three children?

CHAPTER 37

Mrs Evison suffered an exceptionally busy morning. After refuelling the cooker, cooking the men's breakfasts, organising the food and coffee for the men to take with them, the work on the farm had yet to be started. The cows were restless and mooing, impatient for their morning treat in exchange for their milk. The hens, hungry for corn, were clucking; the sheep were bleating in the croft. Her tasks that morning were endless, rendered more numerous and difficult by the adverse weather. Work that she felt could wait was left until later and, satisfied that everything necessary for welfare of the animals had been attended to, she returned to the farmhouse thoroughly exhausted, sighing deeply at the thought of the housework awaiting her.

'Cup of tea, Mrs Evison?' Mrs Markson, asked the instant that she entered, sliding the kettle over the hot hob.

Mrs Evison smiled: 'Oh… Please, Lindsey.' Her spirits brightened instantly and her smile widened, it widened further upon looking about. The pots and pans had been washed and dried and tidied away. But most pleasing was the comforting aroma of food cooking. Mrs Evison removed her coat, hung it on the peg behind the door and slumped in the chair by the cooker.

'Well… You've been busy, I see?' She said, glancing to the pan on the hob.

'It's only a little stew. I hope you don't mind –'

'Mind!'

'I thought the men – the children would be hungry when they returned.'

From where she sat, Mrs Evison reached out; she lifted

the lid from the pan and craning her neck attempted to see what was inside, but depleted of energy and with little inclination to stand, she replaced the lid.

'Well, whatever it is it smells delicious.'

Mrs Markson smiled; she then turned her attention to the steaming kettle. She brewed the tea and allowed it to infuse before filling two mugs. At Mrs Evison's request, she lifted the biscuit tin from a cabinet. The two ladies then settled together by the cooker, warming their bodies, calming their anxieties with tea and home-made ginger biscuits.

'I wish they'd hurry back,' said Mrs Evison, brushing the crumbs from her lips. 'All this hanging about... Not knowing. Still, I expect there'll be much snow to shift and work their way through. It takes time, I know, but it plagues my nerves all the same.'

'Is it far to Blackdaw Cottage?' Asked Mrs Markson.

'A couple of miles. A little further maybe. I don't actually know. I've never been there. Another biscuit?'

'Thank you,' said Mrs Markson, accepting another biscuit and examining it from all angles before biting into it and chewing. 'Mm... Delicious. You must let me have your recipe, Mrs Evison.' The words had no sooner left her lips when a knock resounded on the outer kitchen door, startling both women. But Mrs Evison rose from her chair and hurried towards the door, smiling. The knocking was repeated.

'Only Mrs Brewster uses that door,' she said, unlocking the door and opening it.

The elderly lady bustled inside shivering. 'Took your time, didn't you?'

Mr Evison closed the door: 'You were the last person I expected to see this morning, Mrs Brewster. Traipsing out in all that snow.'

'It takes more than a peppering of snow to keep me shut up inside. And anyway I walked in the tracks left by your tractor… Saw the men set out this morning.'

'Cup of tea, Mrs Brewster? Lindsey's only this minute brewed a pot.'

'Lindsey!' Mrs Brewster responded, searching for the owner bearing the name, frowning upon seeing the stranger sitting by the cooker.

'I'll pour you a cup,' Mrs Markson said, rising from her seat and lifting a mug out from the crockery cabinet.

'That's not mine!' Barked Mrs Brewster.

'The beige mug, Lindsey,' Mrs Evison said, smiling wryly.

Mrs Markson returned the offending mug to the cabinet, retrieved the beige mug and held it up for approval. The elderly lady nodded.

'Milk and sugar, Mrs Brewster?'

'Both,' she replied, somewhat acerbically.

'One spoonful or two?'

'Three,' Mrs Evison intervened, giggling.

The stooped, elderly lady shuffled towards the cooker in ill-fitting wellington boots; the upper rubber slapped her calf muscles and shins alternately as she walked. Mrs Brewster's overcoat was faded and frayed, sporting patches upon patches; it appeared that full value and more had been had from it. She was hatless and her long grey hair was fixed in a bun at the back of her head, speared by a fearsome looking hatpin to keep it in place, which it failed to achieve. Stray strands hung about her face and ears and were wafted aside continually. She unfastened the buttons on her overcoat, revealing beneath a paisley-patterned blue and green pinafore.

'You should wear a hat in this weather, Mrs Brewster.' Mrs Evison said.

'You can keep your hats.' Mrs Brewster said, with a dismissive wave. 'Never liked wearing them,' she said, tucking an insolent strand of hair behind an ear and sitting on the chair vacated by Mrs Evison. 'I wear a hat only to go to church – respect for the almighty.'

Throughout Mrs Brewster's life, no obstacle proved too great a challenge. She was born and brought up on a farm at the end of the nineteenth century. Then, the working day stretched from five-thirty in the morning until ten o'clock in the evening, sometimes beyond. She had never married and had lived in the same village her entire life, boasting proudly of never venturing further than the hills and forests that ringed the village. She purposely steered clear of cities; she had never seen the sea or the lakes and mountains of the British Isles, but her knowledge of local people and events stretching centuries into the past, impressed many. Little escaped her ear or her eye and nothing animated her like local gossip. Her opinion, whether welcome or not, was expressed with candour and enthusiasm. She could be the source of merriment or irritation, calling on people at the most inconvenient hour, when every hinted-at gesture or wish for privacy was blithely ignored. She was interesting to listen to, but listen one must, for once her tongue had been unleashed she spoke loudly over anyone who dare interrupt. Furnished with a pot of tea (in her favourite beige mug) and biscuits to nibble on, she would speak fluently and enthusiastically of any inconsequentiality and make the mundane sound fascinating or dull, depending on the mood and patience of the listener.

Mrs Brewster accepted tea from Mrs Markson, nodding muted appreciation, but the instant she sipped she frowned as though she had taken poison.

'Ugh… No news then?' She said, turning swiftly to Mrs Evison.

'None, yet, Mrs Brewster.'

'Been gone long enough, haven't they? Time they were back!'

'Yes, yes, they've been away for some time now; we'll all be relieved when they return – well, let's hope.' Mrs Evison glanced at the clock. It was twelve thirty. The men had set out to Blackdaw cottage over five hours ago.

CHAPTER 38

Mrs Evison arranged a third chair by the cooker and, after sitting, she reached out and lifted the biscuit tin from the table and presented it to Mrs Brewster.

'What kind are they?' Mrs Brewster asked, straining to see inside.

'Ginger, your favourite.'

'Oatmeal are my favourite,' Mrs Brewster replied abruptly. 'I care nothing for ginger… Ginger gives me wind.' But the instant Mrs Evison began to withdraw the biscuit tin, an arm reached out and a hand seized hold of it. The elderly lady leaned forward and examined its contents.

'They're all the same, Mrs Brewster,' Mrs Evison said, smiling wryly.

'Aye, and great big things – I've little appetite these days.' Mrs Brewster said. But a hand dived into the tin; it was withdrawn clutching a handful of biscuits. 'They're all stuck together, see!' She laughed, her laughter pitching higher. The 'stuck-together' biscuits fell apart onto the pinafore stretched tight across her knees.

Mrs Brewster was a regular visitor to the Evison's home, calling on the family almost daily. She had done so for longer than anyone could remember, sitting always in the same seat by the cooker, in winter or in summer, slurping tea from her favourite beige mug and enjoying several of Mrs Evison's home-made biscuits – whatever kind they might be.

'Well, I must say, I was surprised to see you today,' remarked Mrs Evison.

'I've said already,' began Mrs Brewster, pushing the

last portion of the first biscuit into her mouth, chewing hurriedly and swallowing. 'It takes more than a peppering of snow to keep me shut up inside... Never been one for staying indoors.' She picked up a second biscuit and bit into it, continuing speaking with a full mouth. 'When my father had his farm there was always work to be done whatever the weather. Didn't matter then if it was raining or snowing.' Chewing slowly and thoughtfully, as Mrs Brewster was disposed to do, she burst suddenly into laughter. Mrs Evison, being used to her neighbour's peculiarities, smiled, but Mrs Markson appeared somewhat bemused. After calming her amusement, Mrs Brewster took another sip of tea and turned abruptly to Mr Markson. 'Your tea's not as good as hers.' She said, gesticulating with the half-eaten biscuit, before facing Mrs Evison. 'I had to call... Couldn't rest. Not after learning about Ruth and Morton and, and...'

'And Abigail,' Mrs Evison said. 'Abigail is Lindsey's daughter.'

'Lindsey's daughter! Lindsey who?'

'Markson,' Mrs Markson informed her politely.

'Markson!' Repeated Mrs Brewster, scrutinising Mrs Markson with a concentrated stare, chewing slowly.

'But of course Lindsey wasn't always a Markson,' said Mrs Evison.

'Aye... Your face looks familiar.' Remarked Mrs Brewster. 'And your eyes...'

'Lindsey was a Sanderson before she married Clive,' Mrs Evison went on.

'Clive?' Mrs Brewster looked sharply about.

'Lindsey's husband, Mr Markson. He's gone with the men to help look for the children.' Mrs Evison informed her. 'Mrs Markson was Lindsey Sanderson before she married.'

'Sanderson!' Mrs Brewster repeated, suddenly animated. 'That's a name I do know.' She returned her gaze to Mrs Markson and scrutinised her with greater intensity. 'Aye... Should have known the minute I saw you, those eyes... Unmistakable. I knew all the Sanderson's... Two sisters and a brother, and their names...' She stroked her chin. 'Joyce, Poppy and Brindley.'

'Brindley Sanderson!' Mrs Markson exclaimed. 'You knew Brindley Sanderson?'

Mrs Brewster nodded.

'He was my great uncle. My father's uncle.'

The elderly lady smiled; she lifted her mug up to her lips and sipped slowly while gazing absently in the direction of the biscuit tin.

'Another biscuit, Mrs Brewster?' Mrs Evison said, offering her the tin.

'I'm not one for gorging on biscuits all day,' Mrs Brewster said. 'But if you want rid of them I dare say I can manage another... Brindley Sanderson was your great uncle, did you say?' She asked, turning to Mrs Markson, digesting the name and chewing the biscuit, when a mischievous smile broke upon her lips. Her smile widened and then she erupted in outrageous laughter. 'Well, we all know who Bentley Sanderson is!'

'Bentley Sanderson!' Mrs Markson was aghast. 'You mean he, that man who lives in the woods is also a Sanderson?'

Mrs Brewster fixed her unblinking eyes upon Mrs Markson; she attempted to speak, but laughter prevented her and she pointed again with the half-eaten biscuit.

'You... You and old Bentley...' Laughter again arrested her words.

'Go on, Mrs Brewster, go on,' urged Mrs Evison.

'Bentley Sanderson... You and he are related. Bentley

is Brindley's son,' she said and laughed uncontrollably.

Mrs Markson gasped. Her hands flew up to her face: 'But can you be sure, absolutely sure?'

'There's no doubt about it,' confirmed the gleeful lady.

'But…'

Mrs Brewster's words and laughter reverberated nauseatingly inside Mrs Markson's head; she shivered – not from the cold but from the horror of it all. She picked up her mug and gulped several mouthfuls of tea, watching Mrs Brewster's body shudder to the rhythm of her laughter. The elderly lady composed herself, but only to repeat that which Mrs Markson did not wish to hear.

'It's a fact, Mrs Markson, you and the old man at Blackdaw Cottage are related. 'Who'd have thought it, eh! You, related to a hermit!'

'But surely –!' Mrs Markson began.

'Well, here's news indeed!' Interrupted Mrs Evison, picking up the teapot and refreshing the mugs of tea. 'You then, Lindsey, are Bentley's niece, and Abigail's his great niece.'

'But, but…' Words again failed Mrs Markson. She looked distractedly straight ahead, spooning sugar into her mug, even though she did not take sugar in tea.

'Mrs Brewster knows,' Mrs Evison said. 'She knows everything that goes on in the village, knows all the people… Everything about them.'

Mrs Markson looked up. 'That day – weeks ago, in the greengrocer's shop. He, that Bentley chap, stood staring at me, smiling… The most frightful grin I've ever witnessed… Gave me the willies, I can tell you. Frightened the life out of me. But never did I think –'

'Never thought you'd be related to a tramp, did you?' Interrupted Mrs Brewster, laughing.

'Mrs Brewster!' Mrs Evison beseeched.

The elderly lady, it seemed, took great pleasure from disclosing hidden secrets, conveying news that was disagreeable to the ears of the recipient. The more unpalatable the news, the more Mrs Brewster appeared to enjoy divulging it.

'Bentley must have known all along?' Questioned Mrs Markson. 'This is all too much... Comes as quite a shock... Don't know what Clive'll think when he discovers his wife's related to a... To Bentley.' She turned fidgety and the tone of her voice rose. 'Divorce me, I shouldn't wonder!' She blurted finally, picked up her mug of tea and sipped distractedly.

'He'll do nothing of the sort,' Mrs Evison reassured her.

'And if the children are at the cottage and Bentley realises, what then...?'

'More reason for him to take care of them. After all, Abigail's his great niece, for heaven's sake!'

'Bentley's an intelligent man.' Mrs Brewster said.

'But I thought, thought he was just another wanderer, a recluse.'

'Because he lives differently from you and I doesn't mean he's mad, or bad.' Mrs Brewster said calmly. 'Bentley's a wily old devil, he knows things... Sees things and works things out.'

Mrs Markson set her mug down on the table, took out a handkerchief and blew her nose hard. 'It all too much.' She sniffed. 'Abigail lost in the snow – goodness knows if I'll ever see her alive again. And now I discover I'm related to a, a –'

'For goodness sake, Lindsey, get a grip of yourself,' implored Mrs Evison. 'The children will be fine... The men will be back shortly... Won't dare return without the children.'

'But will they be alive?' Blurted Mrs Markson.

'Of course they'll be alive,' Mrs Evison assured her, even though she could not know that. Her features altered to reflect the possibility, but she strove hard to remain positive and smiled.

'The children'll be fine,' Mrs Brewster said, reinforcing Mrs Evison's hopes. 'Bentley's lived in the forest most of his life, he knows how to survive.'

'*If* the children are at the cottage,' Mrs Markson said. 'Perhaps they never made it there at all.'

'They'll be there,' Mrs Brewster reassured her. 'There's no other place they could have taken shelter in the forest.'

It was not easy being optimistic, but Mrs Evison felt confident that her precocious daughter had been instilled with sufficient good sense and, together with experience gained from working on the moors with her father during adverse weather, she felt sure Ruth would have found shelter. Knowing that, though, did not make the waiting any easier, and the ladies' torment could only end when their daughters and Morton were safely back home and standing before them.

CHAPTER 39

Vargis, after removing his hat, bowed his head and uttered a mumbled prayer. Mr Markson removed a coat from the nail on the back of the door, carried it to the lifeless man and draped it over him. Jack, having never before seeing a dead human, shuffled uneasily; he turned away and scanned the room.

'Dad, look!' He exclaimed, pointing to three mugs on the table by the fireside. 'And Ruth's coat!'

Jet had meanwhile picked up an interesting scent and scurried about the room with his nose to the floor. He nudged open the door to the bedroom and disappeared inside. Instant frenzied barking erupted, which motivated Vargis to hurry after his dog.

'Jet! What…?'

A second dog barked.

'Sputnik!' Jack said. 'It's Sputnik!'

Mr Evison's heart beat hard as he hurried after Vargis. Jack, Mr Markson and Mr Gregory all followed. The bed stirred, the sheets were thrown over and three bewildered faces looked out. Though confused and groggy from sleep, smiles lit up their faces. Sputnik, barking and wagging his tail, raced up to Jack, jumping excitedly at his side.

'Sputnik, old boy,' he said, bending and stroking the animal.

'Oh, Abigail!' Blurted Mr Markson, hurrying to her side. 'Your mother's been worried half to death.' He said, gulping hard. 'I have, we all have.' He leaned over the bed and embraced his daughter.

'I'm sorry dad, but we, we –'

'Well… You're safe,' said Mr Markson, looking to Ruth

and Morton, forcing a smile. 'You all are,' he said, hugging Abigail like he had not done in ages, before holding her at arm's length and gazing fondly upon her. 'Oh, Abigail, we thought we might never see you alive ever again. You must promise never to do anything like it again.'

'I said you and Jack would come, dad,' Ruth said, looking to him. She swung her legs from the bed, stood and was gathered into the safe embrace of her father. Mr Evison smiled as he hugged her. Elsa, disturbed by the commotion, jumped up onto the bed, meowing and looking about. Morton remained on the bed and called the distressed animal to him. Stroking her, he looked anxiously towards the door, expecting his father to enter and berate him for leaving home without discharging his duties.

'Where's dad?' Asked Morton, looking towards Mr Evison. 'Is he waiting outside?'

'He, he's not, Morton. No… He, he couldn't come, he…' Mr Evison answered awkwardly, and then smiled, gesticulating with an open arm. 'Come here, lad.' Morton's face illuminated and he threw back the sheets – startling the cat – and leaped from the bed into Mr Evison's strong arms. 'You, my boy, are coming back to the farm with me and Jack and Ruth.' He said, hugging both children.

'Thank you, Mr Evison,' said Morton, looking to Ruth and smiling. 'We can build a snowman… Tell scary stories and play out on the sledge.'

'Sledging is banned for the remainder of the winter,' returned Mr Evison firmly, chuckling. 'But look… Standing about on the cold floor in your stockinged feet. Find your boots and get them on your feet, quick.'

'Have you brought the tractor, Mr Evison?' Asked Morton, sitting on the edge of the bed, pulling on his wellington boots.

'Aye, lad, and the small trailer to transport you all back home. Jack…' He turned. 'Jack! Where's Jack?'

'He went outside,' Ruth informed him, stamping her feet in order to firm them in her boots. 'Bentley told us a scary story before we went to bed last night.'

'Did he indeed?' Mr Evison responded.

'And he made a pheasant casserole.' Morton spoke enthusiastically until he noticed the gamekeeper's keen eye upon him. Vargis, chewing slowly, shifted his feet and looked sternly to the boy. But Morton, bashful and nervous continued. 'And we had hot orange juice and parkin for supper.'

The gamekeeper cleared his throat:

'S-o-o, that's where all my pheasant's are disappearing, is it? Casseroles!' His voice was stern and his stare severe, but then his features softened. 'Bentley did right… Did you all proud, I'm sure, and I hope you enjoyed the pheasant casserole.'

Morton eyed him with suspicion, but found within him the fortitude to nod, if somewhat tentatively; his two friends nodded also. And Vargis, noticing the children's uncertain faces, was unable to keep up his pretence any longer and broke into a smile, before exploding into laughter, laughter that proved contagious. The gamekeeper was happy that the pheasants he had striven to keep safe from predators since the spring had helped to sustain the lives of the three children.

'Mum's never made pheasant casserole before, has she dad?' Abigail said, turning from Vargis to her father. Her distaste for the man who yesterday slaughtered the crow seemed forgotten about, or conveniently put aside.

'No, no I don't suppose she has,' agreed her father.

'Then I'll deliver a pheasant to your home, young lady – nay damn it, a brace. Then your mother can then roast one bird and make a casserole with the other.' Vargis said, smiling proudly.

'Can I please have a pheasant, Mr Vargis?' Asked Ruth.

'Ruth!' Intervened her father. 'It's rude to –'

'No, madam, you may not,' returned Vargis in his familiar brusque manner. All joy disappeared from Ruth's face, but the gamekeeper was unable to maintain his deceit for more than a few seconds. 'No, madam,' he repeated, with lips quivering, as he attempted to suppress a smile. 'If you're having Morton Rymer staying with you you'll need half a dozen birds.' He said, placing a playful hand upon Morton's shoulder. 'Nay, damn it, a dozen – the boy needs flesh putting on these bones. In fact, every home in the village shall have pheasant. It's likely to be the only meat on anyone's plates this Christmas. The roads will be blocked for days... Weeks! There'll be no chickens or turkeys this year.'

Ruth's smile returned, Morton and Abigail smiled; everyone smiled.

'Thank you, Hector, thank you indeed,' Mr Evison said. 'It's generous of you. I'm rather partial to roast pheasant myself.'

'Me too,' agreed Joshua.

'Who said anything about you!' Barked Vargis. 'You receive more than your fair share of pheasants.'

'Aye, in return for fixing your leaking buckets, buckets fit only for scrap.'

'The buckets have their uses... For carrying corn to the pheasants.'

'Huh, more like sieves. You'll lose half your blasted corn.'

'Wouldn't if you did your job properly.'

The expression on the blacksmith's face hardened: 'Ungrateful blasted goat. Costs me a fortune to fix your buckets – more them than I receive in return.'

Vargis laughed until tears trickled down his cheeks. 'You old fool, you know you're welcome to as many birds as you wish. My cellar has pheasants hanging from every nail from every beam, and no vehicle's likely to get through to collect them this side of Christmas. No sense wasting good meat.'

'But you must give Bentley a pheasant also,' said Abigail, facing the gamekeeper.

Joviality drained instantly from Vargis's face. 'Aye… Well…' He stuttered.

'But you must,' she emphasised.

The gamekeeper shuffled awkwardly, knowing not what to say or do; he looked to Mr Markson for support. But the men were dumfounded and looked questioningly to each other.

'Where is Bentley?' Asked Morton, breaking free from Mr Evison's embrace and dashing towards the door.

'No, Morton! No…' ejaculated Mr Evison.

Morton halted in the doorway.

'But why not?

And, as any child, insistent on doing the opposite of what he or she is instructed, Morton peeped around the door.

CHAPTER 40

An uneasy silence descended, filled only by the wind's mournful howl, interrupted by a cawing jackdaw. Morton sauntered forlornly to Mr Evison's side, looking as though he might burst into tears at any moment.

'I'm afraid your friend didn't made it through the night,' Mr Evison said, taking Morton back under his arm. 'We're all terribly sad.'

'Is Mr Vargis sad?' Asked Morton, sniffing as he glanced to the gamekeeper.

'Aye, lad. Very, very sad.'

The children had lost a friend and were unable to understand why the kindly old man should have been taken from them, denying them the opportunity of thanking him for taking care of them, for entertaining them with the tale of Ivan and Gertrude Murdac on that bleak December night.

'But why did he have to die?' Sniffed Abigail.

'We must all die some day,' Mr Markson said, drawing his daughter tighter to him. 'Death has a habit of sneaking upon us when it's least expected, but your friend was worn out. God decided the time had come for him to take a long rest –'

'But why now?' Questioned Abigail, tears welling up in her eyes. Tears welled up in the eyes of them all, adults and children alike.

'Bentley's at peace now,' Mr Markson continued. 'God's reward for taking good care of you children. He's safe now in heaven, where the wind and frost can no longer torment him.'

'My dad said there's no such place as heaven,' blurted

Morton, sniffing. 'And my dad says there is no God.' He paused and wiped the tears from his face. 'But my dad doesn't know everything, does he? He said Bentley was the devil and it wasn't true.'

'Well, there you are…' began Mr Evison. 'Bentley, I'm sure, must have died a happy man having you three children in his home for company.'

Vargis cleared his throat. 'The forest will be a lonely place without old Bentley creeping about, frightening me half to death.' He smiled. 'We had our disagreements and skirmishes, and harsh words were sometimes spoken, but it was all just harmless banter. I'll miss the old devil, damn it, I will.' The gamekeeper said, blinking rapidly. And he too wiped a tear from his eye.

'But you said you wanted to shoot him,' Ruth reminded him.

'Aye, you're right, young lady. I did say that,' the gamekeeper agreed. 'And there's been times I've felt like shooting him. I've provoked him, and Bentley's provoked me. I've cursed him, and he's cursed me.' Vargis laughed. 'He once grabbed me by my throat… Threatened to strangle the life from me… It was our sport and kept two silly old fools' hearts healthy, but I swear I would never have harmed him and I believe old Bentley wouldn't have harmed me either. I'll miss him, damn it, I will.'

Jack timed his return to perfection, setting the bags of food, flasks of coffee and spare coats for the children down on the bed.

'Right…' began Mr Evison. 'Bentley wouldn't want all this sadness in his home. And we've life here to preserve.' He unpacked the bags, lined the mugs up on the orange box and poured out coffee. When one flask was empty, he took the next. 'Bacon sandwiches?' He mentioned, gesticulating to Ruth. She found the plastic container, prised off the lid and took a sandwich for herself, biting into it and chewing. 'Ruth!' Snapped her father, shaking his head and smiling. 'It's good manners to offer them round before taking one for yourself.'

Ruth shrugged and pushed the sandwiches under Abigail's nose. She took one, as did Morton when offered one. Vargis, Mr Gregory, Ruth's father and brother all took a sandwich, but Mr Markson, cupping a mug of hot coffee between his hands, declined with a smile and a shake of his head.

'Save your crusts for the jackdaws,' said Abigail.

'Save your crusts for the jackdaws!' Drawled Vargis, and then he noticed Abigail glaring in his direction. 'Aye, well, yes. I dare say the birds will be hungry also.'

Mr Evison removed the cap from the hip flask and, without asking, added a measure of whisky to Mr Gregory and Vargis's coffee and to his own, but Mr Markson and Jack both declined.

'To Bentley,' said Mr Evison, raising his mug. The men all raised their mugs and cheered, and the children, looking bewildered, raised their mugs also, smiling as they cheered.

'To Bentley.' The repeated together.

The remaining bacon sandwiches were consumed between the three children, watched over by the grateful and relieved adults.

'Well, I trust you children will have learned something from your misguided adventure,' said Mr Markson, somewhat authoritatively.

'I've learned what bollocks is,' Abigail was quick to inform him.

'Abigail…!' Snapped her father. 'Such language…'

After a brief silence, Vargis laughed out. 'She'll do well enough in these parts… Hardening and adapting already to our forthright ways.'

They all laughed; and Ruth rummaged through the bag, certain that her mother would have included further treats. She was right; and her animation on finding a box of chocolate fingers drew Morton and Abigail closer to her. The biscuits were first offered, with obvious reluctance, to the men. To the children's delight, they all politely declined; and the trio given permission to consume the entire box of chocolate fingers. Chocolate biscuits were ordinarily a treat reserved for special occasions, and then the children might be allowed only two or three biscuits each, but today was no ordinary day. The adults' relief on finding their offspring safe was a cause for some kind of celebration, even it their joy was tempered by tragedy – by a double tragedy.

The coffee was consumed and joviality pervaded the room, giving rise to the suggestion that Bentley's passing had been forgotten. It had not, but eating and drinking is a social occasion that generates high spiritedness, and fatigued bodies were in need of refuelling with energy-giving nourishment to help combat the cold in readiness for the long journey home.

'Coats!' Mr Evison said, after swilling the last of his coffee down his throat. Time was precious and darkness would be upon them soon. 'Come, children, find yourselves a suitable coat and let's get on our way. Put the ladies' minds at rest back home.'

The children, sorting through the coats, disturbed Elsa and she rose, bewildered and meowing, looking to the children.

'Poor Elsa,' Ruth said. 'What about Elsa, dad! She'll starve if we leave her.'

'Better take her with us then, hadn't we?'

'Can we?' Smiled Ruth.

'Aye, I dare say she'll get used to the farm cats, given time – and the dogs.'

'And what about Bentley?' Abigail asked. 'Are we taking him too?'

'No, not today,' Mr Evison said. 'I'll have a word with the vicar, see what's best. Me and Jack'll collect him another day.'

'Will you please feed the jackdaws when you come back?' Said Abigail.

'The jackdaws,' smiled Mr Evison. 'Aye, and we'll bring some crusts for the jackdaws – save the world from freezing over for good.' He laughed, and they all joined in.

Elsa jumped down from the bed and meandered about the floor, meowing. Vargis, after setting his mug down, lifted the cat from the floor and held her in his arms. He looked upon the distressed animal with a degree of tenderness that seemed at odds from a man who appeared happiest when exterminating the wildlife. But Elsa was relaxed in his arms, purring contentedly and rubbing her head up under the gamekeeper's chin.

'Well, there's a rare sight. Hector Vargis caressing an animal – a live animal!' Laughed the blacksmith. 'The poor thing must many times have seen you strutting about the forest with your shotgun, turned tail and fled.'

'Sarcastic, blasted clown.' The gamekeeper said, turning from the blacksmith to Jack. 'Have you a sack we can put her in?'

'No!' Interposed Ruth, alarming Vargis and the cat.

'Eh, what…'

'You can't put Elsa in a sack. She'll be frightened to death. Give her to me.' Ruth demanded, untangling the animal's claws from the gamekeeper's clothing and taking the cat from him. 'I'll hold her.'

'Hold her! But how?' Began her father. 'How can you hold on to the cat and keep yourself safe? It'll be a rough ride back home in the trailer.'

'Here, put this on, Ruth,' said Jack, approaching his sister with an opened coat. 'There'll be room enough inside for both you and the cat.'

'Elsa will be warm, won't she?' Smiled Ruth, securing the cat with one hand, while Jack guided an arm into the coat sleeve, repeating the procedure with her other arm. Ruth held the cat to her chest and Jack buttoned up his sister's coat, leaving only the animal's white head visible. He helped Ruth put on her gloves, pulled a woollen hat over her head and wrapped a scarf around her neck – careful not to smother Elsa – and secured her hood. Morton and Abigail, having found suitable coats, put them on and buttoned them up. The children's clothing was checked and adjusted by the adults. The mugs and flasks were gathered together and stuffed into the bags, and all were ready for the cold journey home.

'It's turned one-thirty already,' said Jack, after consulting his wristwatch.

'Time we were on our way,' Mr Evison said.

The children, though happy to be heading home, were sad that their adventure was over. In the twenty-four hours since setting out, they had experienced much; cut off from their homes by the blizzard and forced to spend the night in the isolated cottage in the forest on the coldest night in years. They had made friends with a man whom some said was the devil. They had shared a meal with Bentley and been entertained by him. They had lost their special friend. It had been an adventure that the children would never forget.

Rescuers and rescued stepped from Blackdaw Cottage into the insipid winter sunshine. The shovels were gathered together and loaded onto the trailer, and the children and men climbed on board. Mr Evison, the last to exit the cottage, checked that the door was secure and then joined them on the trailer.

'Right, let's get going, Jack,' he called out.

Jack crunched the tractor into gear, increased the acceleration and the unit moved slowly away. The children, standing at the front of the trailer, held tight to the wooden rail and looked back upon the lonely cottage, watching until it had disappeared from sight. Without its protective walls, the kindness and compassion of Bentley, the outcome would have been so much different. The three children could easily have become another statistic of the blizzard, as others across the British Isles had on that virulent winter night – indeed, as had Morton's dad.

The trailer with its precious cargo rocked and swayed as the wheels passed over the uneven snow. The wind blew bitter still, whipping the snow up from the ground, flinging the stinging crystals in the faces of the children and adults, but soon they would be home; or so they hoped.

CHAPTER 41

The ladies, sitting in the farmhouse kitchen, waiting and hoping, found respite from their anxieties in Mrs Brewster's propensity for conversation. She spoke animatedly and knowledgeably of all things local or topical, of events current or from the past, of people alive or deceased. Though her eyesight had deteriorated, her mind remained lucid and sharp and no sound escaped her ear. Today, she was especially alert, claiming to have picked up the droning sound of the tractor's engine long before Mrs Evison or Mrs Markson.

'They're back!' She said suddenly, suspending her own conversation.

'Back?' Mrs Evison repeated, turning to Mrs Markson. Both women, listening intently, could hear nothing other than the wind, the sheep bleating in the croft, or a cow mooing repeatedly in the shed. Even so, Mrs Evison's heartbeat quickened; she rose from her chair and hurried to the window, looking eagerly in every direction.

Mrs Markson joined her. 'Can you see them?'

'I can neither see or hear them,' she said, shaking her head. Mrs Brewster must be dreaming… But wait! Now I can… Yes, now I hear the tractor.' Mrs Evison stepped away from the window. Mrs Markson, after scanning the windblown white landscape, followed Mrs Evison to the outer kitchen door. The door was opened and an icy blast greeted the two ladies, but they stood rooted and shivering, impatient to know if the men returned with or without priceless cargo. Mrs Brewster calmed her anxieties with yet another biscuit, joining them at the door:

'Can you see them?' She asked, elbowing her way between the two ladies.

'Not yet,' replied Mrs Evison.

The trio stood together watching, hoping and praying, knowing that any moment joy or despair would break upon them. As the muffled tones of the tractor's engine grew nearer and louder, their heartbeats thumped harder. Then the tractor and trailer burst suddenly into view.

'Wonderful! Oh, wonderful! All three safe,' gasped Mrs Evison. And she and Mrs Markson hugged and jumped and waved.

'Thank God,' shrieked Mrs Markson, removing the handkerchief from the sleeve of her jumper, dabbing her eyes with it. Three smiling children waved back, but Morton's joy was muted as he searched in vain for his father.

Mrs Brewster, observing, remained passive, nibbling a biscuit and chewing. 'I'll put the kettle on,' she said, shuffling away brushing crumbs from her hands. She stepped to the cooker, lifted up the hob cover and slid the kettle over the heat. 'What's cooking?' She asked, noticing a pan steaming on the adjacent hob.

'Lindsey's made a little stew,' Mrs Evison replied, motioning to her friend. 'Come, let's close the door… Shut out the cold.'

'A little!' Exclaimed Mrs Brewster, lifting the lid from the pan and looking inside, replacing the lid noisily. 'You'll spare a spoonful for a poor old woman?'

'For a poor old woman!' Responded Mrs Evison, purposely exaggerated. 'Yes, yes of course we can spare a spoonful for a poor old woman.' She looked to Mrs Markson, shaking her head, smiling wryly.

'I've little appetite these days,' Mrs Brewster went on. 'And it'll spare me the trouble cooking… Can hardly afford to keep a fire lit these days and eat.'

Mrs Markson smiled: 'Well, you weren't impressed by my attempt at brewing tea... Can't imagine you'll have a stomach for my stew!'

Mrs Brewster looked to her and glared but said nothing.

The deaths of Bentley, and Morton's father – whose demise remained to be told to Morton, and would be withheld until the meal had been enjoyed – had saddened the homecoming, but a small celebration was appropriate. The children, after all, were safe and well, in need of a nourishing hot meal after their ordeal.

As fast as Mrs Markson sliced the bread, Mrs Brewster, after buttering a crust and eating unashamedly, picked up the slices and spread on butter the thickness of the bread. She became aware of everyone's eyes upon her.

'No one eats the crusts anymore,' she said, chuckling. 'And I can't abide waste.'

No one had the opportunity of a crust when Mrs Brewster was present.

The plate of buttered bread was placed on the table. The stew ladled into warmed dishes; and the cold and hungry children and adults all took their places at the table. The pity was that Bentley was not alive and able to join them. In the company of his three young friends and their grateful parents, he would have been treated with the respect and compassion he seldom achieved as he lived, been presented with the opportunity to sample the lifestyle he had forsaken, willingly, it has to be said, all those years ago.

CHAPTER 42

If Elsa settled easily into her new home with new friends, she was at times unimpressed by the boisterous play of the sheepdogs, but once she felt that they would do her no harm, she ignored them, and the dogs, unable to provoke a reaction, left the cat alone. Yet one day, about a week later, Elsa disappeared. It seemed obvious to everyone where she had gone and Jack, with instructions to take food to feed the jackdaws, was dispatched to Blackdaw Cottage to bring the cat back home.

On arriving there, he found Elsa sat waiting by the door and the cat, happy to be again reacquainted with a friendly face, raced up to him, meowing. She was transported safely back to the farm and, satisfied that nothing remained for her at the cottage anymore, Elsa never again strayed.

There was no possibility of Morton straying far from the farm, he settled easily into his temporary new home with Ruth, Jack and their parents. He assisted Ruth with her duties about the farm, walking daily with her to the hen-coops to feed the chickens and collect the eggs; he enjoyed the slapdash manner in which the new-born calves took their milk from a bucket. Once the work was done, the pair played on the farm, outside in fair weather, or inside if it was too cold or wet – joined frequently by Abigail. Morton loved life on the farm and hoped that he might be allowed to remain, but his mother was due to arrive in the village in the New Year and she would decide his future.

Mr Markson, it transpired, had not been writing fiction at all. The secrecy he deemed necessary arose because he was busy drafting a volume of his and his wife's families' histories. The finished article had been intended as a surprise present for his wife last Christmas, was planned as a present for this Christmas. Now, with additional information concerning his wife's ancestors being supplied by Mrs Brewster – in return for tea and biscuits – it seemed unlikely that another Christmas would pass without Mrs Markson having her special present.

Christmas was long past before an area of ground in the village churchyard could be cleared of snow and a grave dug in the frozen earth. The churchyard would not have been Bentley's chosen resting place, but a grave accessible to all, it was decided, was the proper place to lay to rest the local hero.

The morning of the funeral was glorious and bright. Everywhere looked pristine under the previous night's coating of snow, and it seemed a travesty that a once-vibrant human being with a passion for solitude and open spaces should be surrendered to the confines of the populated earth of a churchyard, especially on such a beautiful day. Never before had the quaint village church enjoyed an attendance so great for a funeral. Everyone from the village, the surrounding homesteads and beyond, it seemed, had turned out to witness the interment of the mysterious man from the cottage in the forest, offering respect to the man of whom few knew anything at all, and of whom few respected while he lived.

A cruel irony! Hypocrisy!

But isn't hypocrisy endemic? A necessary vice from which no one is absolved, no matter how virtuous a person's claim! While Bentley lived, he was at best tolerated. Few among the hoards who had gathered that morning to mourn his passing had exchanged more than a couple of sentences with the solitary man from the forest. But since that December night, hard-set hearts and mistrustful minds re-examined their consciences and learned to accept what weeks ago would have been unthinkable. Indifference, revulsion and hatred were put aside. Without Bentley, his hospitality and humility, they knew that the lives of the three children could so easily have been snatched from them.

To those whose Bentley's presence had troubled the greatest (born of ill-conceived prejudices, ignorance and fear, as was suffered by the earlier residents of Blackdaw Cottage) the greater appeared their grief. But did Bentley not help fuel those prejudices – rejecting society and choosing to live like a hermit in the solitude of the forest?

Yet all that changed. After finding the children stranded in his home, a space opened up in his heart. A calling as natural as any parent or grandparent might experience was awakened within him. The children's perception of Bentley also changed; he, being no longer the personification of evil, the children warmed to his grandfatherly manner. But is not all humankind related, and the children Bentley found in his home, his children? Was Blackdaw Cottage, Bentley's home, not their home? Was his food, not their food?

Since discovering the abandoned sledge on the hilltop, Bentley's senses were alerted to the possibility that children's lives might be at risk. And like certain species of migrating salmon, after battling upstream and overcoming insurmountable obstacles and odds to reach the place of their birth and secure the survival of the next generation, so too Bentley. Guided through the blizzard to the door of his cottage, and like the salmon, after accomplishing their last great feat, slipping silently into that mysterious new dawn. But unlike the fish, the story of Bentley will remain alive in the minds of future generations, and the tale he told of Ivan and Gertrude Murdac, implanted in the minds of the three children, would be preserved until the end of time.

If Bentley had despised the idea of a public funeral, he would have recoiled at the prospect of being buried in the earth in the village churchyard. His abiding wish had been to lie in the forest earth among the tangle of tree roots, where he could listen eternally to birds; feel the treads of the forest animal's feet on the ground above him.

But a hero must have a public monument, and Bentley's coffin was lowered into the earth in the village churchyard. The three children standing together on one side of the grave – their parents behind – were in sombre mood. Ruth held Elsa in her arms, and Sputnik, resting on his hindquarters at her feet, remained watchful throughout. Morton, standing to her left, fidgeted as he observed the proceedings, glancing fitfully to the mourners. Abigail clutched a posy of snowdrops in a hand and an attached card bore the inscription: 'To grandfather: one fleeting moment of joy, and all too soon it's goodbye. Love Abigail.' The coffin came to rest and she released the flowers into the grave. The approaching vicar, carrying in his hands a wooden receptacle filled with soil, invited the children to each take a handful. Morton looked soulfully to the sympathetic cleric, before filling a hand with the dry earth: Ruth and Abigail did likewise, and the soil was cast into the grave.

The gamekeeper and blacksmith, standing opposite, separated by Mrs Brewster, behaved impeccably throughout. Mr Gregory, contemplative and holding a black trilby in a hand, stroked his moustache with a forefinger and thumb. The sooty residues, having been scrubbed from his face, rendered it impossible to believe that the immaculate figure was indeed Mr Gregory, the same man who toiled endlessly in the heat and grime of his furnace. Vargis was attired in his finest, resolute against habitual chewing, spitting and swearing. After glancing about, he slipped a hand inside the pocket of his overcoat and withdrew it clutching a fistful of feathers; psychedelic streaked feathers plucked from the breast and neck of a cock pheasant. He released them over the grave, leaned forward and watched them float down and settle among the snowdrops and soil.

The vicar began his final lamentation…

There, in that deep dark hole, rests the emptied shell of the man whose memories have migrated heavenward with a spent soul. Dreams long abandoned, dreamed up in idyllic days when the world was new are now all gone, set free into that mysterious abyss. All images captured and scrutinised through those emerald windows are lost; spirited away with the wisdom harvested from a long life. Never will his image again surface on earth, never to again experience the caress of a soft breeze, or suffer the sting of the sun's consuming rays. Life's tribulations will trouble his flesh no more. The feet that trod a billion steps are stopped, his heart has thumped its last, his voice is silent, his world is gone.

The old man of the forest, though, will never be forgotten. Bentley will live forever in the hearts of anyone encountering his story, be remembered as the man who helped save the lives of Ruth, Abigail and Morton on that virulent December night.

Morton received the news of his father's death with fortitude, expressing conflicting emotions, given the uncomfortable times that they shared. The body of Mr Rymer lay in the chapel of rest in a nearby town. His funeral was scheduled to take place the following week. Mrs Evison received a letter from Mrs Rymer thanking her and her family for taking care of Morton. She intended to attend the funeral of her estranged husband. It would be the first time that mother and son had met in almost six months. Morton would have much to tell his mother of his adventure with Ruth and Abigail, of Bentley and Blackdaw Cottage. His wish was to remain on the farm, to live alongside Ruth and her family; Mr and Mrs Evison had agreed that he could stay for as long as the arrangement remained mutually suitable. Mrs Rymer, though, expressed her intention of taking Morton away to live with her. Perhaps she could be persuaded to move back into the village!

Whatever the future held for the three young friends, one eventful episode had ended. Ruth, Morton and Abigail had ventured beyond the boundaries of their abilities on that snowy December day. Next time, there may be no place of refuge and no friendly guardian to watch over them.

The children had undoubtedly learned a valuable lesson, but lessons learned in the flush of youthful exuberance are all too quickly forgotten. Come lengthening summer days and warmer nights, further enterprises would surely beckon. Should the children remain together in the village, who but a clairvoyant could foretell what joy or peril might lay in wait for the adventurous trio?